COFFINS FOR TRAITORS

COFFINS FOR TRAITORS

Gordon Parke

SCRIPTURE UNION 5 Wigmore Street, London W1H 0AD

© Scripture Union 1958
First published 1958
Reprinted in paperback form 1973

ISBN 0 85421 344 9

Photoset and printed in Malta by St Paul's Press Limited

1

On an April day in the year 1711, the Sussex coach was rumbling slowly up Red Hill. A well-wrapped coachman sitting aloft grumbled at the six beasts tugging in front of him, but knew better than to try to hurry them. Inside the coach were three men. Two of them sitting next to each other were army officers resplendent in red— Captain Horatio Canting and Lieutenant Robert Woodruff, both of the Earl of Waye's Regiment of Foot.

Woodruff looked gloomily at the pleasant wooded side of the North Downs that stretched westwards towards the setting sun. He was very conscious of the fact that every mile they travelled was a mile further from London. It was hard that just as he was rising in favour in the court circle through the gracious patronage of Robert Harley he should be whisked away and sent on some wild-goose chase in Sussex. Only last week he had sat next to the great Jonathan Swift in the Cocoa Tree Chocolate House and they had talked as if they were old friends. And now he was sitting next to a bumpkin of a Captain whose military exploits formed his only topic of conversation. Lieutenant Woodruff sighed.

Captain Canting turned irritably towards his junior officer, "Why, Lieutenant, your sighs are more fit for a blushing girl than an officer of Her Majesty. There is more in soldiering than making eyes at milady in Kensington."

1

He paused. Already he disliked his companion, this pale faced, immaculately dressed young officer, who for all his superior airs had never been on the same side of the North Sea as the enemy. He poured as much contempt as he could into his words. Much of his grudge against life came because he considered that the army was being ruined by the fact that influence counted more than merit, especially Captain Canting's merit. And this influence he found personified in the foppish Lieutenant Woodruff.

"Your sighs would have availed you little had you served under our glorious Duke. I well remember at Malplaquet when we drove the French...."

Woodruff sighed again, but for a different reason. He had already heard this story twice before, so while the battle of Malplaquet was being vigorously refought he took the opportunity to examine their fellow-traveller, who, defying the jolts and jerks, was attempting to doze. Woodruff had an irritating feeling that he had seen the man somewhere before, but was unable to place him. A tanned and wrinkled face reminding Woodruff of one of the tame monkeys kept by some of his fashionable lady friends was surmounted by a great horsehair wig some-what askew, and showing underneath the close-cropped grizzled hair of a man of about fifty. Woodruff, scanning his dress, judged him to be a gentleman, but a country one, either not interested in or not versed in the latest town fashions. His clothes were at least fifteen years out of date—a serious fault in Woodruff's eyes.

"And when we charged those Frenchies started to run, and they didn't stop till every mother's son of 'em was back in France," concluded the Captain triumphantly.

"A glorious victory, indeed," observed Woodruff drily. "It's sad your great military talent now lies rusting."

Captain Canting perceived no sarcasm.

"Ah, that's the traitor Harley's work." In this disrespectful manner did he refer to the then leader of the Government. "But our glorious Duke will return and lead us again. And don't forget we have action, at hand, action that may well demand the cool nerve and steady grasp that come from experience."

Woodruff noticed at this point that their fellow-traveller's eyes were now open, but they betrayed no interest in the conversation. Was he deaf? When the journey began he had ignored a polite remark about the weather made by the Captain, so it seemed a possible explanation. Or was he taking in every word that was said? Woodruff wished the Captain would moderate his voice.

Captain Canting tapped a leather satchel on his lap. "In here we have documents which may well lead us to the heart of one of the Pretender's plots, and if that is so the issue will be decided with muskets and cold steel, and away with the pretty words and ways of our fine fops at court!"

This was a theme on which the Captain was never tired of enlarging, more especially as he considered he had a fine specimen of foppishness beside him. Woodruff yawned and shifted uncomfortably on his hard seat. The journey seemed interminable. The six horses which pulled the clumsy old coach were straining hard as they reached the steepest part of the hill. The track they followed (it could not be called a road) was rutted and soft and the unsprung coach lurched jerkily.

"When I've finished this job there'll be some traitors for the gallows," Canting was saying. "Though times are growing soft and many traitors are left unhanged. It's all since the late king brought his strange ideas from Holland. The English way is to hang 'em and not leave 'em to plot fresh treason. There'll be plot after plot till every Jacobite is ten feet from the ground with a rope round his neck. You mark my words."

Certainly it was true that since 1688 successive parliaments had been worried about plots and rumours of plots to restore a Roman Catholic to the throne, and now Anne's Roman Catholic brother, James—"the Pretender" to his opponents and "James III" to his friends and himself—had set up his court at St. Germain in France and was awaiting his chance to win the throne. Spies crossed and re-crossed the English Channel, and there was a large Jacobite party in England which included several eminent members of the Government who professed themselves willing to declare for James III.

What was proving more disturbing to the Army authorities was the knowledge that large quantities of arms were being smuggled into the country from France and were being distributed from a centre in the South to the Pretender's supporters. Patient investigation by a government agent had brought to light some strange happenings in the Sussex village of Lindfield, and it was these that had brought Captain Canting's mission.

"This coach is plaguey slow," grumbled the Captain. "I'll warrant . . ." but here he came to a sudden stop as he was almost jerked off his seat. There was a shout. The coach halted. The passenger opposite sprang up grasping for his sword. He was too late. The door was flung open and a masked figure was on the step covering them with a musket.

"One move, gentlemen, and the good captain is dead." The highwayman's voice was strange, obviously crudely disguised. Woodruff wondered why.

"Step out with your hands above your head."

There was no option but to obey. The three stepped awkwardly out of the coach, where a second masked figure had a pistol levelled at the trembling coachman. Woodruff noticed that the pistol in the highwayman's hand shook. A novice, perhaps, he thought.

"Shall I . . . ?" began Woodruff in a whisper.

"Don't do anything," snapped back the anxious Captain, uneasily eyeing the pistol still trained on him. "We're helpless."

"Helpless indeed," said the highwayman. "Search the coach," he ordered his companion. "One move from the coachman and he'll be a passenger short. Now disgorge your money and valuables. Throw them down in front of you." A small glittering pile fell on the grass. "And that!" he snapped to Canting, who was displaying some hesitation about parting with a small silver snuff-box. The Captain threw it down, but Woodruff noticed that the robber's eyes showed little interest in their silver and only when his companion clambered from the coach clasping the Captain's satchel did his eyes light up.

"What's in there?" he snapped.

"Some ol' papers—nothing else," came a rather disgusted retort.

"We'll take them. The satchel will be useful anyway. Put these in," he said, kicking the pile in front of him. When his orders had been obeyed he backed to where his horse was tethered. The pistol still pointed its wicked snout at the Captain. First his subordinate leapt into the saddle, then the highwayman followed suit.

"A good journey, sirs," came the mocking cry as they dug their heels into their horses' flanks and disappeared into the growing dark. As they galloped off Captain Canting showed his first sign of courage.

"You scoundrels," he roared wildly brandishing his pistol, "You'll be gallows-meat before long." They listened a moment to the faint beat of hooves and then there was silence save for the wild April song of a nearby thrush.

"That highwayman was more frightened than we were," observed Woodruff, as they turned back to the coach.

"Frightened! Us! Speak for yourself, Lieutenant! I hope I shall never be frightened at such a trivial danger. But that robber will pay for it. It will give me great pleasure to supply the evidence to send him to the gallows."

The coach creaked and lurched out of its rut. Their fellow-traveller still said not a word, but Woodruff noted the pallor that had crept over his features, and he noted too how the man always turned his right ear towards the speaker. He must be partially deaf. A depressed silence settled over the coach.

An hour later they arrived at the Five Bells, a noted coaching inn on the Brighton run, where the night was to be spent and where fresh horses would be obtained. The coachman hurried off to give a report to the Sheriff's men about the highwayman, for part of the reward would be his if the robber ever adorned a gibbet.

Captain Canting stumped angrily into the hostelry. Woodruff followed and noticed the respect with which their fellow-traveller was treated by the ostler and the inn-keeper who bustled out to greet him. The three stood talking by the porch and Woodruff was sure he heard "Lindfield" mentioned as he passed.

Following a maid's direction he found their room at the end of a corridor on the first floor. The Captain was slumped in a chair in the very worst of tempers. He glowered at Woodruff as though the Lieutenant were the cause of their misfortune, but said nothing.

Woodruff pulled out a metal mirror from his travelling bag and, having restored his wig to its usual unruffled state, set about brushing the dust of travel from his clothes. With growing irritability the Captain watched. It was the production of Woodruff's powder bag that caused him finally to explode. "Powder! I've been sent on this mission with a young lady! Well," he said changing his tones to sugary sweetness, "you look beautiful now, my dear. Would you honour me by coming and sitting beside me?"

Woodruff was deeply offended. To him it was distasteful to be anything but perfectly groomed. It was hard to bear these slights, but he knew the harsh penalties awarded in the army for insulting a superior officer. He bit back a cutting retort and said instead, "Shall we prepare a report of the robbery, sir, to send to General Livsey?"

"That shows how much you know," sneered Canting. "Do you want promotion? Then forget about reports and keep that tongue of yours from wagging."

"But what hope have we of arresting the gun-runners without those documents? We know General Livsey has a copy. Without them we might as well search for a needle in a haystack."

"Our task will not be easy, but if you want an easy life you've chosen the wrong profession. Get yourself elected to Parliament. In the army, the greater the odds the happier we are."

Thoroughly exasperated, and foreseeing that he would have to listen once again to the glories of Malplaquet, Woodruff hastily interrupted him. "If you'll excuse me, I'm going to dine. Empty-handed we may be, but we need not be empty-stomached."

"Wait," replied the Captain, a smile wrinkling his red cheeks. "Empty-handed we are not." And from a small pocket inside his coat he pulled out a document with a triumphant flourish. "This one is worth all the others."

He handed it to Woodruff who took it eagerly only to see an unintelligible jumble of figures and numbers. The Captain enjoyed seeing his puzzled expression.

"A code, Lieutenant, a French code," he said. "But

we have the key. It gives the arrival dates of the arms consignments at the English coast, and then the arrival dates at a certain place called X—and X, mon ami, (Canting was proud of his skill at languages) is, unless we are much mistaken, Lindfield, our destination to-morrow."

"What are the exact dates?"

The Captain looked slightly uncomfortable.

"Be not impatient, Lieutenant. I have not yet had time to peruse the document in detail, but we have an agent over at Grinstead, one Nicholas Mole, who has supplied us with much information in this matter, and who will decipher this code. We know from him that next Friday a move is expected by the traitors in Lindfield. You will ride over to him as soon as we arrive."

Woodruff was somewhat reassured, but their time was obviously short. It was already Tuesday.

They dined well but silently, and afterwards retired early to bed. Woodruff found it hard to sleep, his restless mind refusing to relax, but the Captain slumbered heavily, doubtless dreaming of Malplaquet.

After midnight Woodruff dropped into a fitful sleep, but an hour or so later he awoke with a start. He sat up and listened. Nothing but Captain Canting's snores. Just as he was lying down again his ear caught a faint shuffling sound on the far side of the room. A rat or ... Woodruff waited no longer. He hurled himself across the floor. There was a growl of surprise and then a heavy thud, and as the cause of the noise dived towards the door, Woodruff grabbed wildly and caught hold of an arm. But his eyes were slow and sleepy, and as he clutched at his prey Woodruff cannoned heavily into a chair. He sprawled across it and his grasp was wrenched loose by a powerful hand. The intruder dashed out along the corridor.

Woodruff picked himself up, and clad only in his shirt rushed after him yelling, "Stop thief!" Reaching the top of the stairs he paused irresolutely, having lost sight of his quarry. There he was met by a somewhat querulous landlord bearing a lantern.

"Now, sir! Now, sir! Calm yourself! What be the trouble? The good folks are all asleep."

Woodruff soon told him the trouble, and grumblingly the landlord led the way downstairs to search for the intruder. A gusty wind blowing in the bar told the story of the escape. The great window there had been forced open, and banged heavily against the wall. Landlord and Lieutenant ran quickly to the window, the landlord to save his glass, the Lieutenant to look out; but the dark deeds of that night were hidden in darkness. He could see nothing.

The landlord promised that the alarm would be given in the morning and Woodruff returned to the room. Captain Canting still snored on.

Anxiously he felt in the pocket into which the Captain had put their last remaining document.

It was empty. Woodruff shivered in the cold night air. For the first time in his life he was afraid.

2

ANDREW Dale strode up Lindfield High Street tasting the freshness of the April morning, and enjoying, on this his eighteenth birthday, an unexpected holiday. He was tutor to Sophia, the fifteen-year-old daughter of Sir Humphrey Pride, of Steadwell Hall, and as Sir Humphrey was returning to Lindfield on that day after a lengthy stay in London, Sophia had been granted a holiday and was even now waiting excitedly at the Tiger where the coach from London was due shortly after mid-day.

Let no one say that teachers enjoy holidays one whit less than their charges. As Andrew strode along the grass track up the High Street he looked the picture of happiness. He was of medium height, and slightly built though his shoulders were broad enough. His carriage was lithe, his step springy. Handsome? Hardly, unless you were willing to overlook a wide, wide mouth and ears that protruded more than is usual. His dark hair was, unfashionably, his own. But he looked carefree and cheerful as he joined the throng outside the Tiger. He could not know that before three days had passed his peaceful pattern of life would be shattered into a jig-saw of separate pieces.

He looked round at the faces he knew well. There was Simon Jackson, the surly innkeeper, standing on his threshold contriving to look more cheerful than usual, and hopeful that the arrival home of the Squire would bring some good custom. Every so often he would turn and scold the effort of the servants who were busied about the inn. There was Sophia, her pretty face aglow with excitement, dancing on tip-toe in the April sunshine, and just as pretty as the April sunshine, while her staid Nanny attempted to soothe her into a more dignified mode of behaviour. And there were the villagers, pleased at the prospect of their Squire's return, but also intrigued by the rumour of a highway robber—for though rumour be a lying jade, she had found many willing ears in Lindfield.

"They say that Sir Humphrey fought six robbers off single-handed!" reported Old Mother Willis, who owned an ale-house down the street.

"And a whole regiment of soldiers were called out," added another, and so the gossip ran on.

"The coach is late," remarked the baker who was profiting by the lateness of the coach as he hawked his crisp bread round the crowd.

"Ay, coaches always are," replied Old Mother Willis. "When they offered me a ride in a coach I said, No thankee. I'm in a hurry. I'll walk."

Andrew joined in the laughter that greeted this popular rather than original sally, and then he stiffened, for his eyes caught sight of Carson Pride, Sir Humphrey's son, standing on the edge of the crowd, his handsome face showing his scorn for those around him.

Andrew hesitated, then, plucking up courage, made his way round to where Carson stood. Carson, for whom the roof tops of Lindfield seemed to have a great fascination, appeared not to see him.

"Why, Carson," said Andrew bravely, "your expression is not in keeping with the brightness of the day nor the joy of the occasion.

Carson gave a slight start as Andrew addressed him, but his face relaxed slightly.

"I would my father's homecoming were not such a public occasion. The cheers of such as these," and he nodded towards Old Mother Willis, " are merely degrading."

Andrew had long realized that Carson's surname was peculiarly apt, but he also knew that this was not the real Carson. He tried again.

"Come, that is not the only reason for your gloom. You have not been to see me for weeks."

"I have been busy in London," interrupted Carson, abruptly.

"And you seem to have lost the power of laughing. You never laugh now. Is it that Mr. Brookestone presses too hard with your legal studies?"

Carson looked thunder, and Andrew sought for soothing words but could find none; then Carson's expression of stiffness dropped from his face as if it were a mask, leaving a bewildered, unhappy look underneath.

"Listen, Andrew," he said urgently. "You must help me. I've something . . ." but his words were drowned in the lusty cry of "Here she comes!"

They listened and heard the steady beat of horses' hooves as the coach rumbled up the hill and round the corner by the Church. The crowd began to cheer lustily. Sir Humphrey was popular, and deservedly so.

Captain Canting looked out of the window of the coach. "Why, this is a fine welcome. General Livsey must have informed the people of our coming. I cannot remember such a reception since we entered Mons."

The coach creaked to a standstill. Captain Canting rose to make a dignified exit, when, to his surprise, a violent tug behind returned him abruptly to his seat. "What . . ." he began angrily, turning only to find that the culprit, their unsociable fellow-traveller himself, had risen and was stepping through the door which one of the crowd had hastened to open. The cheering rose, and then from the step of the coach, Sir Humphrey made a speech suitable for the occasion. This was enthusiastically acclaimed.

The back view which the Squire presented to the enraged Captain was tempting, and it was fortunate that Woodruff was able to restrain him from any rash acts. When the two officers were finally able to emerge, most of the crowd were moving down the street to watch the very latest mode of transport—a sedan chair in which Sir Humphrey was carried with Sophia sitting proudly beside him.

Captain Canting strode across to Simon, the innkeeper, whose ashen face and dropping mouth gave no suspicion of a welcome.

"Are you the landlord of this inn?"

"Aye," replied Simon guardedly.

"Lieutenant Woodruff and I require lodging for at least a week. Lead us to your best rooms."

Simon's obvious dislike of soldiers (a feeling wide-spread in England at that time) and his natural surliness seemed to battle for a few seconds with his love of money. The latter won.

"Follow me," he said brusquely.

"My name, and I should be obliged if you would address me by it," said the Captain, irritated by Simon's disrespectful mode of address, "is Captain Canting."

"And mine is Simon Jackson," came the curt and still disrespectful reply.

They were shown to their room, and though the land-lord might not seem satisfactory the room was; it was not long before they were sitting at table feeling considerably more at one with life.

Captain Canting had by now recovered from the shock of losing the last remaining document. Indeed his confidence in his own ability was so great that he foresaw little difficulty in coming to grips with the gun-runners and outwitting them, and he was beginning to perceive dimly that Woodruff was not without some ability, for all his foppish appearance.

They ate an excellent dinner of poultry followed by blackheart cherry pie and rich hot chocolate, in a silence which was perhaps the result of the superlative quality of the fare.

"They say the Queen eats a whole fowl at a sitting," remarked Woodruff, thinking that the Captain's eating powers must make him a dangerous rival to Her Majesty.

"Aye, she eats well does our good Queen Anne. I hear she has to be lifted from one meal to the next," replied Canting heaving himself laboriously out of his chair.

"Now to business, Lieutenant." He looked round the room, deserted except for a dismal-looking waiter, and then added, "but walls have ears, eh? Upstairs, I think."

They slowly climbed the winding oak stairs to their room, both bending under the low beamed doorway. Woodruff closed the door.

They discussed the position in low voices and eventually agreed that Woodruff should ride over to Grinstead on the morrow to consult their agent, Nicholas Mole, while Canting, who prided himself on his tact, would see what information could be gained locally. Woodruff felt he had already discovered some useful information, but he did not feel disposed to share it with the Captain as yet.

*   *   *   *

Andrew was one of those who watched the sedan-chair as it made its triumphal progress towards Steadwell Hall. At the bottom of the High Street he turned away with a dissatisfied heart. As he did so a cloud blanketed the rays of the fresh Spring sun.

"The uncertain glory of an April day," thought Andrew rather gloomily to himself. His own brightness had been extinguished as suddenly as the April sun. His mind was on Carson, his closest friend since boyhood. Yet now for some months a coldness had frozen the warmth of friendship, a coldness that Andrew could not explain. On his daily visits to the Hall he knew that Carson now did his utmost to avoid him, and if a meeting was inevitable Carson would pass him with but the slightest acknowledgement. It was distressingly different from their happy friendship in the past.

Carson, deferring to his father's wishes, was destined to be a lawyer though he had always longed to join the Army. However in those days it was rare for a young man not to fall in with his father's wishes both with regard to a career and a wife. For several months he had been studying under Talbot Brookestone, regarded by many as one of the most brilliant lawyers in the country on account of his defence of Doctor Sacheverell in the recent London trial. As part of his payment, Sir Humphrey allowed Brookestone the use of several rooms in the East Wing of Steadwell Hall. From time to time Brookestone would take Carson up to London for a week or so, so that his pupil might study the workings of a lawyer's office.

Andrew felt that the beginning of Carson's law studies coincided with the rift in their friendship, and he knew that in spite of his efforts the break had steadily widened. Why, oh why, had the coach arrived just when Carson seemed likely to confide in him again? Carson had then slipped off to welcome his father, and afterwards had vanished though Andrew had searched eagerly for him.

Andrew slowly returned home. Home to him was a small house, red brick and beams outside and nearly 150 years old, where he lived with his old guardian, Daniel Foot, the schoolmaster. Of his parents he knew little.

His mother had died when he was a baby; and his father, of whom he had fleeting memories as a silent but tender man, had died when he was six, when he was left in the care of Daniel. At first the schoolmaster had seemed very old and frightening to little Andrew. Short and thin, Daniel was always dressed in black, and his face was wrinkled and as yellow as the parchments over which he spent so many hours. But Daniel had been kind, and though Andrew had lost his earthly father he learnt from Daniel how to find the Heavenly Father, Who cared for him as his own father had done. Andrew had seen his sincerity and believed him, and though Daniel might be queer to look at and to many people a subject for jesting, it was not long before Andrew trusted him implicitly and, more than that, loved him.

Daniel earned a somewhat precarious living as a village schoolmaster. Money was never plentiful, yet Daniel saw to it that his young ward had the best of everything. He taught Andrew Greek and Latin, so that he knew more than many of the local young gentlemen who pursued their studies at Oxford; he had taught him how to ride and fence (for Daniel was a man of surprising parts), and Andrew was considered as good a swordsman as any in that area; but most of all he had taught him to love the Bible—"God's Word to us," he called it. How Daniel treasured the great family Bible they read together night by night!

One night when Andrew was studying Virgil, Daniel had gently taken the book from his hands.

"Herein," he had said to the surprised Andrew, "is man's wisdom—fine and beautiful, but mortal." Then he had picked up the Bible. "And herein is God's wisdom, great and glorious and immortal; and yet, Andrew, there are many who think man's wisdom is wise indeed, but God's wisdom is foolishness. Mark well what I do read, Andrew, and then I would that you answer what I ask."

Thus it was always with Daniel Foot. He was a true shoolmaster, for he was for ever asking questions. So he had turned the pages of his beloved Book and read these words: "For the preaching of the cross is to them that perish foolishness, but unto us which are saved it is the power of God." He had turned to Andrew. "Answer me this, but do not answer too easily. Is the cross to you foolishness, or is it the power of God unto savation?"

Andrew had for some years trusted in the Saviour Who had died for him on the cross, and he need not have answered the question, for the expression on his face must have told Daniel all he wanted to know; but he did put his answer into words. And great was Daniel's joy.

Carson also had been a pupil of Daniel, for Sir Humphrey had considered that the schoolmaster's brilliant teaching outweighed his personal oddities, and under Daniel's guidance Carson too had come to trust in the Lord Jesus Christ as his Saviour. Many a time since then it had been to old Daniel that he had turned for advice.

Andrew arrived at the cottage and went slowly into the hall. It was sombre and chilly. This was where Daniel used to hold his school. An old desk was still there where Andrew had spent many toilsome hours, and there hanging above the dais where Daniel had sat was the birch, a reminder of painful episodes to Andrew, and now merely a happy hunting-ground for spiders.

Andrew resolved to tell Daniel of the events of the day, and was about to tap on his door when he heard voices inside—first the quiet voice of Daniel, and then the strangely agitated voice of Carson. Andrew stepped back, not wishing to interrupt, but as he did so the door was flung open. Carson stepped out, pale and tense.

"Carson..." began Daniel.

Carson turned in the doorway.

"No, no. Let me think! Let me think!" he cried in a taut voice. "I must work this out for myself." And turning, he hurried past Andrew without a flicker of recognition and rushed from the house.

Andrew stared after him for a moment and then entered the room. The old schoolmaster was sitting motionless at his desk. He seemed not to notice Andrew's entry. His lips moved. "We must pray for him," he muttered, "Pray he has not left it too late."

"Left what too late?" broke in Andrew.

Daniel looked up wearily. "Nothing, Andrew. I should not speak so; it ill becomes one who knows the mercy of God, who knows the story of the dying thief on the cross, to say 'too late'."

Andrew could make nothing of this. Irritated and baffled, he stood till Daniel took pity on his bewildered expression. His tone was serious as he spoke again.

"I have just heard a story, Andrew, that had I not heard it with my own ears, I would never have believed."

"Yes, I saw Carson coming out. What did he say? Why did he come? It's a long time since he visited us," Andrew gabbled out the words in his anxiety.

"Aye, but I trust 'twill not be long before he comes again. But there's danger, Andrew, Carson is surrounded by danger now."

"What was it all about?" cried Andrew. "What danger?"

"There are no words of man can save him now. 'Tis only prayer," said Daniel, appearing not to hear Andrew's question. The young man glared in exasperation.

"What was it all about?" he persisted.

Daniel's eyes lost their faraway look as he glanced at Andrew.

"I would I could tell you, Andrew; but Carson would not speak till I had promised never to disclose the story without his consent. I promised because I thought I might help him. Perhaps I was wrong."

Andrew's mind was awhirl. What was Carson doing? He was about to release another torrent of questions when he remembered Daniel's promise. It was no good.

Daniel spoke again. "Evil is afoot, Andrew. In the last half-hour I have learned too much."

The frustrations of the day were making Andrew sulky. No one told him anything. He burst out,

"I can't see why there should be all this mystery. Anyone would imagine it was a matter of life and death."

Old Daniel remained strangely silent.

3

ANDREW was an avid reader. What money he had to spend went on books, and his greatest heroes were those he had come to know through his reading. Copies of the new magazine, *The Spectator*, already littered his small room (tidiness was not one of his virtues), a well-thumbed copy of *Pilgrim's Progress* lay open by his bed, but that night it was to the Bible that Andrew turned.

He found himself reading the story of Moses and of his indomitable leadership of the Israelites during the weary years in the desert. His imagination was fired as he read the story of that rugged old man who kept going in face of every discouragement. He took courage from it. After all, *his* worries were but small ones.

Andrew's main anxiety was not that there was danger, as Daniel, who had been unusually strained, had suggested, but that he would be kept in the dark. What was the danger? From whom did it come? In what way was Carson involved? Surely his old friend could not mean them any harm? Daniel had been strange that evening, had refused their wonted game of chess, and had merely sat silently staring blankly at the wall and shivering though the evening was not cold. Andrew had been glad when it was time to come to bed. He took courage from the Bible reading and as he prayed he knew that, come what might, the One Who had saved him would keep him.

He lay down, but sleep would not come. He walked across to the small window—no glass, but a parchment shutter. He pulled the latter down. A silver light flooded his bare room and the cool air refreshed him. Outside the moon was high above Scaynes Hill and the dark trees were silhouetted against a deep blue sky. A dog barked from the farm of his friend and neighbour, Peter Virley, and from much nearer a bird rustled in a bush and flew squawking away. Another rustle drew Andrew's eyes to the bushes that lined the rough track that led to their cottage. There was a large animal there. Straining his eyes Andrew distinguished a moving shape. It was a man!

More than that Andrew could not tell, for the intruder was making good use of cover, and he was approaching the cottage. Andrew's heart missed a beat. He waited till he heard the stranger attempting to force the door, and then Andrew went swiftly across his room in his stockinged feet, fumbled in the corner for the sum total of his inheritance from his father—a sword—drew it from its scabbard, unlatched his door and slipped out and then down the narrow staircase. A rending noise below told him the door had been forced. The intruder was inside!

In his excitement Andrew trod too heavily. The stairway creaked protestingly. As he flung open the door at the foot of the stair Andrew was sure he heard a scuffle. But the hall was empty. The front door swung open and the breeze was rustling some papers at which Daniel had been working. They fluttered from the table to the ground. Otherwise all was still. Andrew, his sword at the ready, peered into the dark corners of the hall. There was no one. He ran to the door and looked out at the still scene. He could see no one, though he well knew the intruder might still be lurking near.

A disappointment crept over him. He had failed. The

danger was still near and still unknown. And then he thought of the small store room at the far end of the hall. It was just possible that the intruder might have taken refuge there. Without much hope he strode across the hall and flung open the storeroom door. The blackness yielded nothing to his eyes. He prodded forward with his sword and felt the pile of firewood he had collected the day before. He turned away disgusted that his first adventure should end thus, when a noise behind him jerked him half round before a sickening blow stunned his senses and he fell forward unconscious.

It was not till the silver moon gave way to the golden sun that his limp body was found by old Daniel. When Andrew opened his eyes his old friend was kneeling before him dabbing his head and forehead.

Andrew hastily closed his eyes. The light hurt them. His head throbbed.

The joy in Daniel's heart was great when he found that Andrew had suffered little more than a headache. He offered up a prayer of thankfulness to God and Andrew had recovered sufficiently to join in the "Amen".

The old man listened carefully as Andrew told the story of the night before.

"The villain has left us little to recognize him by," said Daniel. "But your arrival may have interrupted him. We have suffered nothing but a broken latch."

"And a broken head," put in Andrew wincing as he gingerly felt his wound.

"Grieve not over that. You are young and a broken head is but a lesson."

"A lesson!" exclaimed Andrew, somewhat aggrieved.

"Aye, a lesson to teach diligence, diligence when searching a room."

It seemed to Andrew a poor time for sermons, but so glad was he to see Daniel in better spirits that he even smiled.

"But why did he come, Daniel?"

The old man shook his head. That was indeed the question. There was little of value in the cottage. The thief, if thief he were, had left no richer for his pains.

Two fresh trout, caught by Andrew the previous twilight, and rich coffee made a good breakfast for them. Warmed by the food Andrew drew some satisfaction from the feeling that at least he was in the battle now. The first blow had been the enemy's; the next would be his.

But not only was his head aching; so was his self-esteem. He was somewhat nettled by the taunt about not showing enough diligence. As he washed the plates under the pump he made up his mind that he would make Daniel eat his words. He would track down the intruder.

He examined the broken latch with care, but it afforded him no clue beyond that the intruder had a strong instrument probably made of metal, and Andrew's throbbing head had already informed him of this.

Next he tried the store-room, and there he was more fortunate. Kneeling on the musty floor where the intruder must have knelt he found by his foot a wedge of slightly moist red earth, shaped, it appeared, to fit between the heel and sole of a man's boot. Andrew's eyes glistened. Lack of diligence indeed! He had a clue. There was only one spot near Lindfield where soil like that was found, and that was in a quarry in a large spinney on the estate of Sir Humphrey Pride. Andrew had played there often enough as a boy with Carson as his companion. He gave a slight start as he thought of this. Why did every train of thought lead him to Carson?

"I will not be straight home after lessons this afternoon, Daniel," he said as casually as he could. "I have some business I must attend to."

Daniel forbore to comment as he watched Andrew go, but he noticed that whatever this business might be, it apparently required a sword.

Meanwhile at the Tiger, as the two officers were finishing breakfast, the seedy looking waiter sidled up to the table and dropped a sealed paper in front of Captain Canting.

"A special rider brought this last night," he announced dully, "but Mr. Jackson gave me orders not to disturb you then."

The Captain was just about to rebuke the waiter for such slackness when he noticed the message came from General Livsey. Promotion, perhaps? With trembling fingers he tore at the seal which gave way easily (suspiciously so in Woodruff's eyes). Canting's face fell as he read the contents. He dropped the message to the table and stared blankly ahead. Woodruff picked up the paper and read, "The copies of the documents which you hold concerning the Lindfield case have disappeared. It is suspected that they have been stolen. Thus it is imperative that you guard the documents well." There followed the General's signature.

Canting laughed bitterly. "He's probably sold them to the Jacobites. Half the London Generals would sell out to St. Germain if there was enough money in it."

"He's not the only one who has lost them," came an unwelcome reminder from Woodruff.

"No, but we lost ours fighting," retorted the Captain, who already had in his mind a picture of the robbery that was imaginative rather than factual, "not sitting in comfort exchanging compliments with the ladies."

Woodruff reflected that though the Captain's remarks were exaggerated, there was probably some truth in them. Fom the start of the expedition he had noticed a lukewarmness and inefficiency about the arrangements which suggested at the least a lack of enthusiasm on the part of their superior officers. Woodruff also knew that as in Parliament so in the Army there were notorious Jacobite sympathizers, and it had already occurred to him that failure rather than success in their mission might well be the object of the organizers. After all, the choice of the leader of the expedition was surprising, to say the least, and Woodruff was modest enough to realize that his career to date offered little evidence of military ability.

The Captain was speaking. "This makes your expedition to Nicholas Mole vital. He alone can give us the information we need. You must ride over to Grinstead at once. We will hire a horse here."

No one recognized the urgency of this more than Woodruff, who suspected that whereas inefficiency might be the case with *their* plans, the opposite was true of their opponents. His experiences later that day were to confirm this.

"And you must take down from Mole all the information he has. I'll investigate here. The villagers in a small place like this probably can tell me much that will be useful."

Woodruff doubted the Captain's abilities in this line, but refrained from comment. Through the windows they saw the ostler leading a large but bony piebald horse.

"Ah, your horse," said Canting.

"Yes," replied Woodruff without enthusiasm. There was that about the look of the beast which caused him some misgivings. They went out.

"A powerful-looking horse," observed the Captain, standing well back.

"'E's a beauty, sir, is Cromwell. Only needs the right 'andling. Keep on good terms with 'im and 'e'll do all you wants. The trouble with the young gen'l'man last week was 'e didn't know 'ow to 'andle 'im."

Woodruff mounted his steed, which stood sullenly still. He patted him hopefully and gently dug his heels in his flanks. Apart from an ominous twitch of the ears there was no response. However, the ostler, thoughtfully armed with a hazel switch and possibly feeling that the reputation of the stables was at stake, gave Cromwell a hearty cut behind.

This time Cromwell's reponse was immediate. He half reared and then bolted up the road past the Church towards Grinstead, with Woodruff displaying an equestrain skill he did not know he possessed. Before long, however, he and Cromwell had come to a reasonable understanding, and he began to enjoy his gallop along the rutted lane which meandered through woods and over grassland. This adventure would be an antidote to the boredom and dissatisfaction which, he was forced to admit in his more honest moments, he had felt latterly in much of his London life. He galloped confidently. He would be at Grinstead within the hour.

Captain Canting watched Woodruff's dramatic exit and was just about to recount to the ostler the tale of his famous ride with the cavalry at Oudenarde when he discovered that the ostler had gone. Now for his investigation. He decided he would not take a horse himself. He looked down the High Street. It was deserted. Then the sound of footsteps behind made him turn. He saw a large figure in clerical garb and with wig askew coming hurrying through the churchyard towards him. It must be the Vicar. The Captain decided that the Vicar would make an excellent person with whom to start his investigations, unless of course he had any Jacobite leanings, in which case he must be placed high on the list of suspects. Glowing with pride at the cunning he was about to show, he approached the oncoming Vicar and with a dignified bow prepared to introduce himself.

Unfortunately the Reverend Thomas Bysshe, Vicar of Lindfield, was short-sighted, and even more unfortunately perhaps he refused to admit this fact and so he abjured the use of spectacles which were becoming increasingly popular. The Vicar, though vaguely conscious of something red in front of him, did not slacken speed as he emerged from the churchyard. He presumed that the red something would move. He was wrong. The impact of his stomach on the bowed head of Captain Canting was considerable. Canting staggered back losing his hat in the process. The Vicar gasped and came to a standstill.

It was fortunate that the Vicar was a good and amiable man. If our portrait seems to paint him as somewhat eccentric, let us remember that he truly spent his life in the service of his flock, for whom he toiled and prayed in an age when many vicars resided abroad and had never even visited the parish that supplied their income. He found in Lindfield much indifference, and the church was but sparsely filled on Sundays. It was discouraging, as also was the sight of his lovely church of All Saints crumbling into a ruinous state for lack of funds. And it was on this theme that his mind had been running when he met the Captain.

Canting's tongue, as we know, could wag at a merry pace, but the tongue of the Reverend Thomas Bysshe could wag at an even merrier one. Before he had fully recovered the Captain found himself being hustled into the church with the Vicar talking nineteen to the dozen. He was indeed receiving information about Lindfield, but none of it had the remotest bearing on any treasonable activity.

As they examined each crack in the masonry and each flanking pillar the Vicar rambled on rapidly, touching on the beauty of fourteenth-century glass, the difficulty of collecting tithes, the scandalous cost of having bells repaired, and the bad state of the vicarage.

The Captain made several attempts to break into this monologue, but in vain. He stared moodily round the once beautiful church. His eyes fell on a memorial slab on the wall which bore the inscription:

> So As you ARE so
> Once were wee As
> Wee are so you
> must bee.

It took Canting some time to work this out, and he was not much cheered by it when he had done so. However, the Vicar was now leading him through the church porch again. In a short pause the Captain began hopefully, "Have you heard...."

"And this graveyard is more a pasture for the farmers' cows and pigs than consecrated...."

Captain Canting gave up, and as they reached the road he bade the Vicar a hasty and thankful farewell. The Reverend Thomas Bysshe hardly seemed to notice, but swept on down the village street still muttering about the iniquities of the time.

Captain Canting wiped his brow. The April sun was warm. He decided he had earned a drink, and entering the Tiger went slowly upstairs to his room, which the waiter whose behaviour had riled him at breakfast was just leaving. The waiter gave a slight start as the Captain appeared.

"Just a tidying up, sir," he said as he slipped past.

The Captain shouted an order for a drink after him and entered his room. Then he stopped. His chest had been moved. His boots had been moved. The room was not the same. It was not merely a matter of tidying up—in point of fact the room was far from tidy. The clothes he had left strewn on the bed still lay there. He walked across to his chest where most of his belongings were stored. His suspicions were confirmed. He remembered exactly where he had put his best wig—on top, at the right-hand side; and there it was under his shirts at the other end.

At that moment the waiter re-entered with the drink, his shifty eyes avoiding the Captain's.

"Someone has been in this room," thundered the irate officer. "Going through my belongings."

"Only me tidying up, sir," said the waiter nervously.

"Did you open this chest of mine?" demanded the Captain, advancing.

The waiter put down the drink on a table.

"I was just tidying up, sir."

"'Pon my soul, I've a mind to run a sword through you if you don't give me a direct answer." The Captain seized the waiter by the coat. "Did you open this chest?" And he emphasized each word with a vicious tug at the waiter's coat.

"Oh, 'ave mercy, sir!" screamed the waiter. "No, I never touched your chest. I was just tidying up, sir."

The Captain flung him back through the door.

"Send the landlord up," he ordered.

" 'E's out, been out all morning, sir."

"Send him up when he returns."

"Yes, sir." The waiter disappeared thankfully enough. The insolence of the morning had disappeared.

The Captain went thoughfully over to the chest, and was about to examine the contents when he saw a folded sheet of paper attached by a pin to the inside edge of the lid. It was addressed to Captain Canting at the Tiger. Snatching it down he opened it and read,

> *In the desk of the cottage of Daniel Foot*
> *there is that will interest those who seek*
> *to rid the realm of spies and traitors.*
> *God Save the Queen.*

4

ANDREW found his hours with Sophia particularly tedious that morning, and it was almost certain that Sophia found them likewise. His nocturnal adventure had not improved the Tutor's temper, and his mind was so full of what was to follow the lessons that he treated Sophia's efforts at Latin grammar with an unwanted harshness, while the girl, excited by her father's return after such a long abscence, found Virgil little to her taste and was surprised and hurt by the ill-temper of Andrew.

The minutes dragged by. Next door he could hear Sir Humphrey in deep conversation with Lawyer Brookestone, Carson's tutor. Andrew disliked the lawyer mainly because he felt that it was since his association with Carson that his friend had become strained and cool towards him.

As Andrew had arrived that morning Brookestone had been talking with Carson in the hall, and he had caught a glimpse of Carson's face before he turned and went up-stairs. It was a ghostly white, and Carson's handsome face, drained of its colour and desperate, kept coming between him and Virgil.

Lawyer Brookestone had then turned towards Andrew. His face seemed to Andrew to be the personification of cunning. His eyes were sharp and grey and set far apart in a broad forehead. His nose was long and sharp and his lips were thin: Surely if a fox took human form he would look like Lawyer Brookestone, thought Andrew as he entered the hall.

"Ha, the tutor to our lady," the lawyer had said. "And he carries a sword." His voice was a perfect blend of surprise and contempt. "Faith, schoolmastering must be a more dangerous occupation than when I was young. The instrument of the schoolmaster was then the birch."

Andrew had been stung to retort wildly, "Indeed, sir, I am but a tutor to oblige Sir Humphrey. My sword is for other business. My life will not be spent in the schoolroom, nor yet in studying musty wills," he added defiantly.

Brookestone smiled drily. He never laughed.

" 'Tis clear indeed the birch is no longer the schoolmaster's weapon. Young puppies were trained to show respect in my day." And the lawyer had turned abruptly and walked away while Andrew stood there blushing. He had said too much. How right James was when he called the tongue "an unruly member". Andrew had wished he had heeded the warning of the Bible. Brookestone might well be powerful enough to persuade Sir Humphrey to dispense with Andrew's services.

Sixty minutes' break was allowed to Andrew and Sophia for dinner, which was served to them in the room in which they worked. After a somewhat frigid silence had been thawed out by the natural warmth of their friendship, they chatted about domestic affairs. Sophia, too, was worried about Carson. Her high-spirited brother had become almost a stranger. She told Andrew that that day Carson was to ride to London to resume his work at Brookestone's office. It was clear she shared Andrew's feelings about the lawyer. However, she could give no reason for her dislike and said that her father regarded Brookestone with the very highest respect and would not hear a word said against him.

They returned to their books, but at last the hour of release came. Andrew left the house and followed the drive while he was still in view of the windows. And then as soon as he had rounded the bend he slipped off the path, through the bushes to the fields of young wheat on the way to the quarry. As he did so a gloom raced across the fields and engulfed him as a dark cloud passed across the sun, but he.strode on cheerfully. However his resolution did suffer slightly as scrambling through a hedge he saw the spinney of larches looking dark and sinister in the sombre light. Even as a boy he had felt there was a mysterious atmosphere surrounding the place and now that feeling, stronger than ever, made him hesitate. And then the scene was transformed. The sun shone out again and Andrew walked on briskly, surprised at his fears. After all, he was probably on a wild goose chase.

Then he noticed a strange thing. He found he was following some cart tracks, deep ruts and heavy hoof-marks in the soft earth, all of which were obviously recent. The tracks were leading towards the spinney. Andrew glowed with excitement. He could think of no reason why carts should pass this way save at harvest time, and that was eight months back. Could there be a connection between these tracks and the intruder the previous night? In his excited state of mind Andrew had no doubt about it.

As he neared the spinney he halted under the shadow of the hedge and gazed intently at the spinney with its slender larches and great bushes of briars. There seemed to be no sound or movement save for the gay scamperings of the rabbits in and out of their burrows, and this too suggested that no one else was about. Andrew continued more cautiously and remembering his experiences the night before he kept a wary watch behind. His determination to keep in cover meant he had to leave the cart tracks he had been following. He reached the spinney and slipped in quietly with his hand on the hilt of his sword. But there seemed to be none to see his impressive entry save for the scurrying rabbits. Andrew hurried along a twisty and now overgrown path which he had made long ago to the edge of the quarry.

At first it seemed to be just as he had always known it, the reddish sides falling sharply to the marshy hollow at the bottom, which was luxuriantly carpeted with lush green weeds. At the far side from where he stood the slope was more gentle, and that was the only approach for the unadventurous. Andrew and Carson had always made descents and ascents by clambering on the steep sides at the cost of many scratched legs and torn garments.

As Andrew surveyed the scene from behind a bush he saw that the steps which he and Carson had cut to a cave half-way up on the left-hand side were still there and in excellent repair. The cave was a remarkable one. It was narrow at the entrance, but broadened out to about ten feet and ran about thirty feet into the cliff. Carson and he had always used it as their base and hiding place in times of trouble, and a very excellent friend it had been to them.

Suddenly Andrew's casual gaze became alert as it fixed on the easy slope at the far end of the quarry. Surely there were tracks there—cart tracks! Forgetting his caution, he hurried round the top of the quarry towards where he had seen the tracks. There might be some good reason for the tracks through the field, but why should any cart come to this disused old quarry? Excitement welled up in him again as he squelched over the springy tufts of grass and weed.

Yes, he was right. They were cart tracks, and where they ended the ruts were nearly two feet deep. Clearly it had not been possible to take the carts any further for fear of their sinking right up to the axles.

But why bring a cart to the edge of a marsh, which was

difficult to cross even in the driest season, and at any other time almost impossible? Andrew knew this from sad experience. And then two yards from where he stood he spotted a dark patch in the marsh. He prodded with his sword. To his surprise it was stone. He was almost certain it had not been there a few years back. He leapt nimbly on to it and then saw a line of these stones running across the marsh to the steps which he and Carson had made up the steepest side to the entrance of the cave. The stones were large and firm.

Striding easily across, Andrew soon reached the steps and realized why, at a distance, they had appeared so well preserved. They had been re-dug, and that by expert hands. They were larger and safer than his and Carson's amateur efforts, and his eager eyes saw footprints and fairly recent ones on each step.

Shortly Andrew's footsteps were added to the others as he sprung up towards the cave. He found it hard to believe that the quarry where he had had so many boyhood adventures was now the scene of an adventure of serious reality—just how serious he did not know. A sudden crashing sound in the spinney brought him to a tense halt on the last step at the entrance to the cave. He looked back, listening intently. The larches sighed reassuringly in the April breeze. It must have been a falling branch.

Andrew slipped through the narrow entrance to the cave. His eyes, unaccustomed to the gloom inside, saw nothing for a moment, but gradually he could make out dark shapes on both sides of the cave. Groping forward, his hands found what seemed to be a wooden case and sliding downwards they felt another beneath. Andrew soon found that these cases, shaped much like coffins, were stacked in tiers of three round all the walls of the cave. He reckoned there must be nearly fifty of them.

But what was in them? With exciting pictures of gold, silver, and sparkling jewels in his mind, Andrew tried to prize his sword under the lid. After three fruitless attempts, rendered more difficult by the lack of light, he gave up and using his hands examined the coffins more closely. It was hardly surprising he had been unsuccessful. He found that each coffin was tightly embraced by three iron bands, which, as far as Andrew could feel, had no breaks in them. He tried to lift one, but after raising it a few inches lowered it hastily and thankfully. If that coffin contained a body, the body must be of a veritable Falstaff, Andrew decided. He stabbed peevishly at the cases, but achieved nothing more than a few scratches on the woodwork.

He was just considering his next move when a noise of crashing undergrowth outside jerked him to attention. The noise continued, and to Andrew's dismay he seemed to distinguish the occasional note of a man's voice.

With his heart thumping wildly he crept to the entrance and peered cautiously out. His worst fears were realized. Down the slope from the fields plodded two sturdy cart-horses pulling an empty wagon, and leading the horses were two roughly clad men wearing high seaboots, doubtless as a precaution against the marsh.

Mastering a flood of panic, Andrew thought fast. He had no doubt that whatever the business of these men was, it was illegal. He suspected it was smuggling, which he knew was rife along the Kent and Sussex coast. Duties were high in the days of Queen Anne, and Customs officers few.

If it was smuggling, then these men were playing for high stakes—death could be the penalty if caught—and Andrew realized that they were not likely to allow anyone who discovered their secret to live to tell it. He shuddered slightly.

From his cramped position he attempted to assess his enemies' armoury. He could see no swords, but the larger of the two men had a pistol tucked in his belt.

This pistol decided Andrew's course of action. If they

had had no firearms he would have left his shelter then and attempted his escape as he had done in friendlier battles, but that pistol made this scheme too risky. He would present an easy target at a range of little more than ten yards.

He must stay, then. They would be certain to find him, but Andrew reckoned that getting him out would present them with a considerable problem. The narrow entrance to the cave and the steep approach provided an excellent defensive position. Then when night came the darkness would come to his aid and give him a good chance of slipping away. The plan had the added advantage of allowing Andrew to examine his enemies more closely. He watched them as with much labour and occasional exclamations they turned the horses and then backed the wagon as nearly as they dared to the marsh. Andrew felt sure their accents did not belong to Sussex; his guess was London.

The larger of the two, who was addressed as Joe, appeared to be the leader. With a wave of his arm he motioned his companion to follow him across the black stepping-stones. Joe had a broad red face crowned with red hair. Two small pale blue eyes were set far apart and in between was a great flattened nose. His appearance was made the more unpleasant owing to a complete absence of eyebrows. He was big, but lithe enough as he sprang over the stones. He looked every inch a fighter, and a vicious one at that. The man behind was insignificant in comparison, but his face was hard. No quarter could be looked for. Andrew felt sick as he waited. Joe started to grunt up the steps.

"Stay where you are!" Andrew commanded sharply, relieved to hear the firmness of his voice.

Joe stared up in amazement but all he saw was the business end of a sword protruding from the darkness of the cave. Joe's brain did not move fast. Hitherto the plan had always gone so smoothly he had not considered the possibilities of any hitch. He stopped.

"There's someone in that cave, Joe," came the helpful growl of his companion from the step below.

"There is, Jesse," Joe agreed. He reached for his pistol. He might be slow of thought, but he could be quick enough when it came to killing. "Who are you?" he shouted up.

"Someone who has been here more times than you have," replied Andrew, who was beginning to enjoy himself as he realized the strength of his position.

"And someone as won't never some 'ere again," replied Joe after a pause. "We'll blow yer brains out."

"Come gentlemen, then. Blow away. I fear neither you nor death. I think you cannot harm me, and I know death cannot." Andrew *was* enjoying himself.

Joe with his pistol raised took a step upwards. Five feet above his head, the sword suddenly flashed in the setting April sun.

Joe with his pistol raised took a step upwards. Five could not see his target, and before he could see his target he must encounter that flashing steel. He turned and made a sign to Jesse. They both began to descend and made their way cautiously across the stepping-stones. When they reached their horses, who were munching happily at the lush grass, Joe and Jesse seated themselves on the wagon and held a council of war. Andrew having ascertained by quick glances what they were doing was content to keep behind cover. He reckoned that time was on his side and that night would prove an ally in his escape plans.

Joe glowered up at the dark mouth of the cave, and after some thought and some mutterings suggested a plan to Jesse. The plan was simple enough. He, Joe, would place himself on the side of the quarry opposite the cave where he could easily cover the mouth with his pistol. Then Jesse would approach up the steps with a stout staff. As soon as the defender of the cave came forward to meet Jesse, he would present a target at which he, Joe, would be able to shoot.

"But what about me?" protested Jesse, to whom the idea not commend itself, "I'll be between 'im and you."

All Joe's assurances about his marksmanship failed to convince Jesse.

The sun was sinking when Joe finally produced an acceptable plan. They would pretend to leave the spot altogether, lead the horses away and tether them in the field, and then lie in wait for Andrew who would presumably make a dash for it.

"You win this time," shouted Joe to the mouth of the cave. "But if we catch you 'ere again we won't let you go."

Andrew heard their ostentatious preparations for departure, and saw them slowly leading their horses off. He was not taken in. He well knew that they could not afford to let him escape, and that this was no retreat but merely a ruse to draw him from his vantage point. He considered the possibility of slipping quickly away then, but Joe might have remained hidden in those bushes. No, he must wait for darkness to fall.

Joe *had* remained in the bushes, and was strategically if somewhat damply placed, not twenty yards from Andrew. Jesse, having tethered the horses, slipped quietly back armed with a stout cudgel. He took up a position not far from Joe.

Dusk fell and a cold vapour rose from the marsh. Jesse shivered. Bull frogs croaked and plopped about round him. In the distance could be heard the lowing of Sir Humphrey's cows, as they were driven out from milking.

Joe shifted uncomfortably and squelched as he shifted. He cursed silently.

Andrew was not aware of their positions, but he was certain they were there. He would have liked to try again to break open one of the coffins, but it was too dangerous to leave his post. Once they gained the entrance to the cave they gained all. He decided that as soon as it was dark enough he would make his attempt. He prayed and found comfort in it. Hitherto not unnaturally the thought of death hardly crossed his mind at all, but now that he was face to face with it he did not feel afraid. The trimphant words of Paul, "O death where is thy sting, where, grave, thy victory?" ran incessantly through his mind.

He looked out. All was dark, though he could have wished it darker. Now for it. He grasped his sword more firmly, and prepared to leave the cave, which had sheltered him so well.

5

WHILE Andrew was playing his lone hand in the quarry, Captain Canting was also active. He had stared at the note for some time, before walking to the door and yelling for the waiter. The same trembling waiter responded to the call with an alacrity that had not been noticeable at breakfast that morning.

"Yes, sir," he whined as he hurried up.

"Have you seen this before?" Canting thundered, waving the note under his nose.

"That, sir, no sir, never in me life, sir!" replied the waiter.

"Who is Daniel Foot?" demanded the Captain.

The waiter did not appear at all surprised at the sudden change in the conversation, but whereas Woodruff would have noticed that, the Captain did not.

"Daniel Foot, sir? 'E's an old schoolmaster. Lives in a small 'ouse over on the 'eath."

"What do you know about him?"

"Me, sir? Nothing sir! Only sees 'im when 'e goes to Church on a sabbath like."

"Aha, Church, eh?" said the Captain. "You may go, and don't forget I want to see the landlord as soon as he returns." Captain Canting, sore at his fruitless morning, was willing to suspect the Rev. Thomas Bysshe of anything, and in his mind he began to imagine the church as a nesting ground for the conspirators, with the Vicar and this schoolmaster, Daniel Foot, as the leaders. Well, he would soon shatter their plans. With ill-founded confidence he saw himself as Major Canting receiving grateful thanks for his services from General Livsey himself. Now for action.

Having found out from the now obedient waiter exact information about how to get to Daniel Foot's house, he swaggered out and down the street, a not unimpressive figure in his well-filled red uniform with his sword dangling by his side.

Leaving the street, he followed a path muddied by April's rains towards Haywards Heath. The afternoon was bright, and Captain Canting looked forward to telling Woodruff how quickly he had picked up the trail.

Daniel's house stood about twenty yards back from the path on the edge of Haywards Heath, a wide stretch of common land.

Captain Canting thundered at the door and listened. He heard some shuffling sounds and then the door opened and there stood Daniel Foot.

"Daniel Foot?" inquired the Captain roughly. He always was at his most soldierly in the presence of those whom he felt to be weaker than he.

"Aye, good Captain. What news do you bring?" replied the old man, who was distinctly worried, having seen Andrew depart armed with his sword when ostensibly his duties were no more than teaching Latin to a girl. Daniel had faced many a danger in his life without any anxiety, but he found it hard not to worry over his young charge, Andrew.

"News?" said the Captain. "My news is that I come to search the house in the name of the Queen." He pushed his way past the amazed Daniel and stood in the middle of the old schoolroom. His eyes lit up as he saw a schoolmaster's desk.

"What's in there?" he demanded.

"The desk? Why I hardly know. 'Tis years since I used that. A few books, perhaps, a...."

"Aye, and some books can teach us much," sneered the Captain. "Why, you grow pale, Master Foot. I warrant there's much of interest in this old desk." His observation that Daniel had grown pale was not accurate. In all the years Andrew had known his teacher and guardian he had never so much as seen a tinge of red on his wrinkled face. But the Captain was not to know that. He flung the lid of the desk dramatically open.

There were some musty dusty old books. Rather disappointed the Captain picked one up, and then gasped with amazement. He dropped the book and plunged his hand into the desk again, drawing out a silver snuff-box. It was Daniel's turn to be amazed.

"'Tis mine!—It's my snuff-box. I would know it out of thousands!" The Captain's mind began to work. The highwayman had stolen it from him. He knew Woodruff had always suspected that that highwayman was more concerned with the papers related to their mission than with their gold and silver, but he had always poohpoohed the suggestion. Now he began to revise his ideas. He turned fiercely on Daniel.

"Where's the rest of the loot? Sold already?" he snapped.

"I don't understand you, Captain. That silver object, a snuff-box, I believe you said—my eyes are not what they were—is unknown to me."

"That will not do," said the Captain rudely. "This is your cottage and your desk, and snuffboxes do not walk, I think." He laughed unpleasantly. "You would be well advised to tell me all you know about it while I am in a merciful mood. I am considered quite an expert at sword pricking. We found that in Belgium it often helped French prisoners to remember what they thought they had forgotten."

"I know nothing about it," replied Daniel quietly.

The Captain glowered angrily. Certainly it was hard to believe that this shrivelled husk of a man was either of the two robbers. He tried a fresh line of approach.

"Do you live alone?"

"No. Andrew Dale, an orphan who was entrusted to me by his parents, lives with me."

"And how old is he?"

"Eighteen."

"Eighteen, eh? A manly age. Is he a good horseman?" The Captain was priding himself on his subtle approach.

"He knows well enough how to ride."

"Ah, and where was he two evenings back?"

"Two evenings back? Why—he was here—reading and playing chess."

The Captain laughed. "Chess! Nay, I think he was playing some bigger game than chess. Ha! what have we here?" While he had been questioning Daniel, the Captain had been walking round roughly handling anything that interested him. He had reached the small alcove of the schoolroom where Daniel used to study. The table and indeed the floor were littered with papers, and it was a handful of these that Captain Canting seized. The Captain himself was not a literary man and never read for pleasure. All writers he regarded with some suspicion. He had no doubt that these were treasonable documents and began to read them eagerly. A bewildered expression crept over his face. He looked towards Daniel who stood by the smouldering wood fire.

"What are these?" He waved the crumpled papers.

"Treat them with care, I pray you, Captain. They are some notes I am writing on the 1st Epistle of St. Peter." The Captain's bewilderment remained.

"Some notes on what?" he demanded.

"On the Bible," said Daniel.

The Captain looked incredulous. Could anyone waste so much time and paper on such a thing? He looked at the papers again but could make nothing of them. It must be a code, he decided. An idea came to him.

"If these are some old papers about the Bible let us put them to good use. The cottage is cold and damp. Let us use them to feed the fire. They will make a merry blaze."

A gleam shone in Daniel's dark eyes. His voice which had been humble enough now rang with authority.

"Lay down those papers, Captain. They are the work of years, and I shall not stand by and see my work wantonly destroyed. You may search the cottage and examine all that is in it, but those papers you shall not touch!"

In spite of himself the Captain laid down the papers and stared at the puny figure by the fire. He could not understand it. If these papers were merely about the Bible, surely no man would set such a high price on them. No, they must be, as he had suspected, a code. His hand reached for his sword. A little sword-play would bring this schoolmaster to his senses.

"Take care, take care. I am not one of your brats for your 'you shalls' and 'you shall nots'. If I say these papers will be burnt then burnt they shall be. Stand back from the fire!"

Whether Captain Canting meant to carry out this threat is hard to say, but defiance from someone weaker brought out the worst in him. Anger surged up. The successive irritations of the past few days had all pricked him on to his present unreasoning fury. He suddenly felt an urge to kill this little man who had stolen his snuff-box and was now daring to defy him. He advanced towards him sword in hand, and then stopped surprised. Old Daniel was also holding a sword. Captain Canting had decided that a few pricks with his sword would make this withered old schoolmaster more submissive. And now here he was standing ready to fight. The dark eyes which stared at him steadily out of the pale face made him strangely uneasy. He resolved on action.

"Drop that sword!" he shouted.

Daniel did not stir.

"Very well, sir." The Captain lunged forward, and as he did, up flashed Daniel's blade. The swords clanged and slithered together. The Captain thrust again and again the blow was parried.

"You fool!" cried the Captain. "A few fencing lessons will not save you from a soldier who has spent a lifetime of fighting." And again he attacked. Daniel nimbly turned the blow and slipped from his back-to-the-wall position.

Now the Captain was a good swordsman; he thought himself to be a brilliant one and he was in his prime. His opponent was old, and for many years had not touched a sword apart from instructing Andrew. But had the Captain met the ghosts of some who had died at Sedgemoor or in the tragic events that followed he might have learnt of a small middle-aged schoolmaster whose valour and skill with his sword almost turned a lost cause to a triumphant one, and through whose valour many supporters of the young Duke of Monmouth had made good their escape. The schoolmaster's name was Daniel Foot, and one of those who had Daniel to thank for their escape was John Dale, Andrew's father.

But the Captain was not to know all this. All he knew was that just when he seemed to be close to a triumphant start to his mission, he was being mocked and hindered by the silence of a schoolmaster. He would make him talk, or die. Death, to one who had fought at Malplaquet, was commonplace enough.

With fury Captain Canting renewed his onslaught. The old schoolroom rang to the clash of steel and the heavy breathing of the Captain, for he was expending much energy. Daniel's defence gave nothing away, and though he retreated slowly before the battering of the Captain's sword, he kept the light of the window behind. He knew that his fading eyesight needed all the help it could get. The Captain, red in the face, swung and thrust, but each blow was checked and turned. At last a mighty thrust from the Captain seemed likely to go home, but at the last second a clash of steel announced that Daniel had turned it past him. So sure had the Captain been of the success of the lunge that all his weight was behind it. Unbalanced, he stumbled forward. His sword crashed against the wall and dropped to the ground. Captain Canting found himself on his knees.

Daniel stood back as the Captain, red and panting, regained his feet.

"A slip," he said. "This plaguey floor. Have you learnt your lesson yet, or do I have to teach you more?"

The faintest of smiles played round Daniel's lips, but he said nothing.

"How did you get that snuff-box?" demanded the Captain, who felt that the whole situation was becoming ridiculous and unprofitable, and yet he found himself incapable of devising any plan. His experience in the past had taught him that tongues usually wag when steel flashes close enough, while if he arrested the old man on suspicion much trouble might come if he had made a mistake. In the Army he had learnt the value of having a superior officer's authority before committing yourself in any way. The Army way—and the easier way in the Captain's experience—was to kill rather than arrest. And then the old man might well give much trouble as a prisoner, especially as the Captain had no suitable prison in mind. For some thirty seconds after he had asked the question the Captain stood there irresolute. Daniel did not reply. His mind too was working, but at a considerably quicker rate. He suddenly realized he knew the answer to the Captain's question, but he knew too it was an answer he would never give.

"How did you get that snuff-box?" thundered the Captain.

Old Daniel looked suddenly tired and frail. "You must find the answer to that question yourself," he said wearily. "I cannot give it."

A sudden blind fury rushed into the Captain's mind. He was being mocked—no one must mock him. In a mad rage he dashed forward lunging at the old man. Taken by surprise, Daniel had not time to raise his sword in defence. The thrust went home, piercing Daniel's thigh. He fell forward and lay still at the Captain's feet, his arms flung out in front, his face on the ground. By his leg there welled out a pool of blood.

The Captain stared without a flicker of emotion. He was used to this.

"The old fool!" he muttered. "He will not cross swords with me again." The Captain's powers of self-deception were remarkable. It would not be long before he would be regarding this as a magnificent victory against the odds.

He went once more round the cottage, but found nothing that could in anyway be connected with the highway robbery, or indeed the traitorous plot which he had been sent to uncover. He returned once more to Daniel's papers and attempted to read them. Finding them as incomprehensible as before he stuffed some roughly in his pocket. Perhaps Lieutenant Woodruff with all his schooling could make something of them.

He strode across to the door, and turned to take one last look at the body. Daniel lay silent and motionless.

"You'll be here when I return," was the Captain's

farewell as he stepped out in the April sunshine. A sense of depression hung over him as he tramped back towards Lindfield. He tried to throw it off. Woodruff should be back from Grinstead soon with all the information they needed. It would probably be enough to put a rope round the neck of that old man—that is, if he had not already saved the hangman a job.

He reached the Tiger. There was no sign of his subordinate. "What can he be about.... ? I should have done the job myself. He's probably bungled it completely or been robbed on the way back."

He wandered moodily out into the High Street. It was deserted. And then he remembered the ale house. He had noticed it earlier and had decided to pay a visit. He had had some good ale out in Flanders. He found it was a way of forgetting any worries, and though he knew not why exactly, he was a worried man.

Under a notice which advertised the power of the ale house products a skinny hand in faded paint pointed the way through a dark alley. The Captain groped his way through and came into a yard surrounded by tumbledown old shacks of huts. Outside dirty children were playing in the last rays of the sun, and two mangy dogs sniffed optimistically round in search of something eatable. A noise of chatter and laughter guided the Captain to his destination. He entered the largest of the huts, a barn-like building with rotting thatching and crumbling old beams. At the roughly-hewn benches and tables sat the clients of Mother Willis. Old and young women, unkempt and uncaring, were jostling and shrieking together while a small knot of men were huddled round a table in deep concentration—gambling. At a small table at one end Mother Willis dispensed her liquor from a great earthenware jug.

At the entry of the Captain a sudden silence fell upon

the ale house. The children outside followed the Captain and gaped through the open door, the gamblers turned momentarily from their game, and the women, those who were not too drunk, stared with interest and suspicion.

Mother Willis rushed forward as to an honoured guest, and it was not long before the Captain was seated at a table deep in conversation with his hostess and some of her more favoured clients. At first she was at pains to emphasize the respectability of her establishment, but when she discovered that this did not interest him a whit, she merely concentrated on keeping him well supplied with alcohol while he refought the battle of Malplaquet. As he drank he found his cares evaporating and his memory of the past became more imaginative with every glass.

It was not long before he had let fall the object of his visit to Lindfield. His audience was now larger. Even the gamblers were interested, and Mother Willis, who knew he had still plenty of money jingling in his pockets, was most concerned that there should be none when he left.

"You're wise, Captain, to be sure, or you would never have been picked for such a job," said Mother, filling his glass again, "and brave too, is he not? The way he won the battle of Mulblackett for the good old Duke!" In the enthusiastic murmur of assent that greeted this, sharp ears might have detected an element of jeering, but the Captain's ears were by no means sharp by now.

"Thank you, good lady, thank you. I think indeed my wisdom and bravery are highly esteemed by the friends who know me," and he grinned round at the bystanders. "I include you among those, good people," he cried. Another cry of approval greeted this. Mother Willis leaned forward. "You are so kind, Major, to us humble folk that we would to do you a good turn." Her cunning little eyes gleamed at her prey. "Would you be wishing to know the name of one of the traitors?"

At these words, the Captain tried to pull himself together. "It is the duty of all sub .. subjects," he began.

"Of course," leered the hostess, "'tis a dangerous secret, a valuable secret." She laid great stress on the word "valuable".

The Captain stared vacantly around for a moment and then thrusting his hand in his pocket pulled out a crown which he dropped on to the table. He laughed heartily. "As valuable as this, eh?" he almost shouted.

Mother Willis' scrawny claw snatched the coin.

"Now the secret, the valuable secret," said Canting.

"You shall have it." And Mother Willis bent even closer over him. "Watch Simon Jackson, the landlord of the Tiger. He's a sly 'un, and he's no lover of Brandy Nan."

"S-S-S-Simon Jackson, my landlord...?" began the Captain—but he was destined never to finish the sentence. He stopped as a great hush fell across the barn. There framed in the doorway stood Lieutenant Woodruff, white and breathless, his redcoat mud-spotted, his boots without their shine. His eyes were scanning the occupants of the barn in the dim light. His taut face slackened with relief as he distinguished the redcoat of the Captain from the group around his table. He strode across. The by-standers fell back and the Captain looked up dazedly. Woodruff gave a smart salute and the Captain's effort to return it brought sniggers from the interested spectators. Mother Willis was debating whether to offer a drink to the new-comer, when he spoke and the tone of his voice told her there was little to be hoped for from him.

"I have urgent news, sir," he rapped.

"News?" murmured the Captain. "What news?"

"It's private, sir. If you would care to step outside."

Captain Canting rose unsteadily to his feet and began to stagger towards the door. A ribald cheer went up from his fellow-drinkers. Thoroughly disgusted, Woodruff walked beside him, guiding and steadying him.

"What news? What news?" demanded the Captain as they started up the High Street towards the Tiger. Woodruff glanced quickly round. They seemed to be alone. He began in a low voice, "I reached the house of Nicholas Mole at Grinstead at eleven o'clock."

"Speak up, Lieutenant. Don't whisper. And what news had he for us?" asked the Captain, attempting to pull himself together but slurring his words badly.

"He had no news, sir," came the quiet reply. "He was dead. He had been shot in the back not long before I arrived."

6

It was while Woodruff was telling Captain Canting the results of his mission that Andrew was slipping down the steps of the quarry. He had decided he must risk going down. To climb up in the dark was difficult and if he made one slightest noise he would be a helpless target for Joe's musket. He reached the last step noiselessly. So far so good. His sharp eyes could detect no sign of Joe or Jesse, but he judged rightly that they were probably hiding behind the low bushes at the open end of the bog. That certainly was the obvious line of escape and therefore the one he could not take. He must now trust to the marsh to save him. He had waded through it before now. He prepared to slip into the marsh.

Low clouds blanketed all but the faintest glimmer of moonlight, but even as Andrew put his foot into the marsh his sword, hitherto his friend, betrayed him. Joe saw an unmistakable glint in the moonlight. He leapt up, and calling Jesse to his aid, made good speed across the stones. Desperately Andrew tore his feet from the clinging marsh, but he could not move fast enough.

"Got you now," shouted Joe in triumph, as he levelled his musket. The distance was less than twenty yards. He couldn't miss. He pulled the trigger. Click! A misfire. The reason was easy enough to guess. He had allowed the powder to get damp. Joe cursed noisily and shouted to

Jesse to get round to the top of the quarry. Andrew, thankful to leave spongy mud, reached the edge and began to scramble up the quarry side which rose steep and dark above him.

Jesse hurried round the rim of the quarry to where Andrew would reach the crest. In his hand he bore a short cudgel. As Andrew panted upwards stumbling and slipping in his haste he realized he was by no means free yet. His sword was a hindrance as he climbed and there was Jesse above in a strong position. Desperation speeded his thoughts. He was almost at the top. A few feet above stood the dark figure of Jesse gently swinging his club.

"One more step and I'll knock your brains out," said Jesse unpleasantly.

Andrew had to act quickly. He could hear grunts and small landslides of stone behind which told him that Joe was in pursuit. He made a wild spring for the top and landed precariously on the ridge. Jesse swung viciously at his head. Grasping for a firm hold, Andrew ducked just in time. The cudgel whistled over his head. As he sprang up Jesse aimed a stabbing kick which, if it had landed, would have sent Andrew the shortest route back into the marsh. But it never landed. Breathless and tired as Andrew was, he was agile enough to avoid the heavy boot. He leapt to his feet, sword in hand. Jesse stepped back. He had no taste for a fight now, nor indeed had Andrew who wanted only to escape without blood on his hands, but as he turned to run into the darkness a sickening blow hit the back of his head. He stumbled forward dazed, his sword dropping from his hand.

Joe, who realized more clearly than Jesse that Andrew must not escape alive, had used his musket to good purpose. Seeing Jesse defeated he had flung it desperately but accurately. Andrew, half stunned, rolled on his back. Joe charged in for the kill, but almost instinctively Andrew thrust out his feet which met Joe amidships. With an agonized roar he crumpled. Staggering to his feet Andrew ran and ran.

Through bush and briar he crashed, and as he ran his head throbbed painfully the refrain "Run and hide". He knew he must find a temporary hiding place in the spinney. There was little cover across the fields, and once he was seen he doubted whether he could outrun his pursuers in his present condition. The fox's burrow! His boyhood knowledge of the spinney was standing him in good stead. Years ago Carson and he had spent a day trying to dig a fox out of its hole. The result had been no fox, but a sizable hole. If he could keep his lead this hole might save him, but his head was throbbing and his legs were aching and behind he could hear the heavy tread of Joe and Jesse crashing after him.

Brambles tore at him, branches whipped his face. Andrew felt his pursuers were gaining as he reached the spot where the hole should be. Where was it? For a split second which seemed like minutes to Andrew he thought he must have lost his bearings, but then he saw the hole almost hidden now by briars. All the better. He dived in.

Not five seconds later Joe was on the scene followed by Jesse, who had picked up Andrew's sword.

"Where did 'e go?" shouted Joe hoarsely. "'E's disappeared. Stop that noise! Stand still and listen." Jesse obeyed but the silence told them nothing. Andrew was afraid that his heavy breathing would betray him, but he need not have worried. Joe and Jesse were breathing even more heavily.

"'E must be 'idin' 'ere," said Joe. "You take the bushes that side and I'll take these."

It was fortunate for Andrew that his hiding hole was in the portion allotted to Jesse, for Jesse's enthusiasm for the night's adventure had waned long ago, and his main interest now was how much money he could make on his newly acquired sword. His method of searching was to swing casually at the bushes with his cudgel as he tramped round muttering to himself all the while. Even this method gave Andrew some anxious moments as the cudgel crashed through the briars above him, the impact causing the thorny tentacles to tear painfully at his bare flesh. Then Jesse tripped in the continuation of Andrew's fox-hole. His mutters became more voluble.

"Found 'im?" called out Joe.

"Nearly broke me leg," returned Jesse. "'E's not 'ere," he added, standing within two yards of the prostrate Andrew. "'E's probably miles away by now." Joe was coming to the same reluctant conclusion. He came over to Jesse.

"A certain gentleman is not going to be pleased with tonight's work," he said. Jesse did not answer.

"It will be better if 'e knows nothing about it," he said firmly. "Got that, Jesse?"

A grunt from Jesse showed that he had.

"We'll go and fetch the horses, Jesse. We won't be finished till midnight now."

And that was the last Andrew heard, as they tramped off towards the quarry. He lay still for another quarter of an hour. He knew the dangers of underestimating his enemy. Then he slipped cautiously out of his hole and stealthily made his way out of the spinney. There was no sign of his pursuers, who were indeed busy harnessing their horses half a mile away. Andrew began his two-mile trudge home across the fields.

He saw no one. The people of Lindfield preferred to do their travelling in the light in those days. Andrew's head throbbed with violent pain, but he scarcely noticed it, so great was his exhilaration at having thrown off his pursuers and having disentangled some part of the mystery which had begun to enshroud him in the last twenty-four hours.

Daniel's cottage was in darkness. This surprised Andrew, for Daniel rarely retired to rest from his studies without liberally burning the midnight oil and it was now but ten o'clock. He opened the front door and stumbled as his foot tripped on something—a body. Andrew knelt down in horror. It was Daniel. He hastened for a lantern. With trembling hands he fumbled with the tinder box. The spark caught and gradually the room was filled with a dull yellow light. Kneeling in the blood, Andrew felt the old man's pulse. It still was beating faintly. Andrew sent up a prayer of gratitude. Tenderly he turned Daniel over and placed his head on some sacking. His eyes flickered open but closed again without a glimmer of recognition. Where was the wound? Feverishly Andrew felt for the rent in Daniel's clothes. It was a deep thrust, but the bleeding seemed to have stopped.

He ran to the pump with a bucket, and with the water cleaned the wound as far as he could. He knew he must get him to bed, but wisely he decided he needed help to move the old man.

The hour was late but he knew he had a friend near at hand who would help. Half-a-mile across the heath lived Peter Virley, once a pupil of Daniel and now a small but prosperous enough farmer. His father had died recently, and Peter was now owner of an eighty-acre farm, on which he lavished all his enthusiasm and diligence. His had been the first farm in Sussex on which Jethro Tull's famous drill had been used, and his wheat and barley always fetched the best prices in London. He was a silent man, who loved his farm more than anything in the world, but Andrew could think of no one better at a time of crisis. Leaving Daniel as comfortable as he could, he ran across the field by the dim light of the lantern slipping in the ruts of Peter's carts. He reached the old farmhouse where Peter lived alone.

Andrew hammered at the door. Some cows lowed, and it was probably this more than the knocking that brought Peter quickly to the window.

"Who's there?" called Peter drowsily, but with a note of sharpness.

"It's Andrew. Listen! Daniel's been wounded. He's lying on the floor and I can't move him easily. Will you help me?"

But he need not have continued. After hearing the first words Peter had disappeared from the window and shortly he was beside Andrew, a stout staff in his hand. As they went Andrew explained the situation and admitted he was quite mystified as to how it had happened. Who could have visited the cottage and who would have wanted to attack old Daniel? Peter's replies had been no more than grunts till he suddenly stopped. Impatiently Andrew turned round. Peter began slowly, "I was sowing Eight-acres this afternoon and I saw a Redcoat going up to your cottage. An officer, I think. And then just as I was thinking it was milking time, I heard strange noises coming from the cottage."

"Strange noises?"

"Well, I didn't think them strange then. 'Twas steel against steel and that's common enough with you and all your fencing and such."

"A Redcoat officer. That must be one of those who arrived at the Tiger yesterday. Now why...?" He stopped suddenly and grabbed Peter by the arm. They were near the house now.

"Look!" he said. "A lantern!" And he pointed to a

dim glimmer of light flickering through the window of the cottage.

"Well?" asked Peter uncomprehendingly.

"I left the place in darkness. I took the only lantern."

"Put yours out, then." A note of authority came into Peter's voice and he gripped his staff more tightly. "It may be a friend but...." He left the sentence unfinished as they crept forward to the window. Cautiously they peered in. One look was enough.

"It's the Redcoat officer," Andrew whispered hoarsely. "Give me your staff, Peter. I'm going to settle scores!"

The Redcoat officer, however, was not the one seen by Peter Virley earlier that afternoon. It was Lieutenant Woodruff.

The blood on Captain Canting's coat had led him to ask a series of questions. The Captain's answers had not always been coherent, but in the end he had dragged the story of the Captain's afternoon from him. The story was hardly accurate, but Lieutenant Woodruff realized that whether Daniel Foot was a traitor or merely an innocent sufferer at the hands of the bungling Captain he must himself investigate. The shock of his frustrating and fruitless mission to Grinstead and the confirmation of his growing suspicions about the uselessness of his superior officer were two of the factors that were bringing about a great change in his outlook.

At first he had regarded this posting as little more than an amusing adventure, a tale of Army inefficiency that would delight his coffee-house companions. But it was as if a light-hearted chase of a deer had brought them face to face with a tiger. He had learnt in twenty-four hours that their ill-equipped, inadequate mission was pitted against a powerful and ruthless enemy. This realization transformed a careless patriotism into a real one. He who had laughed at the good but not always wise Queen was now ready to defend her to the death.

That evening another experience had shaken the Lieutenant, when he had examined carefully the papers which Canting had taken from Daniel. He had hoped his sharp eyes might discover some code hidden in the writing but he soon discovered this to be a false hope. Nevertheless there was something about the writing that had riveted his attention. He had continued to read, and the words he had read had burned themselves on his mind.

"The whole course of a man's life out of Christ is nothing but a continual trading in vanity," Daniel had written, "running a circle of toil and labour and reaping no profit at all. Let the covetous and ambitious declare freely, even those of them who have prospered most in their pursuit of riches and honour, what ease all their possessions or titles do then help them to; whether their pains are less because their chests are full or their houses stately or a multitude of friends waiting on them with hat and knee. And if all these cannot ease the body, how much less can they quiet the mind. You that are going on in the common road of sin be persuaded to stop a little and ask yourselves what is it you seek or expect in the end of it."

And here there seemed to be some pages missing, but a torn fragment which the Captain had found in the bottom of his pocket contained these words: "If the promise of God and the merit of Christ hold good, then they who believe in Him and love Him are made sure of salvation. Sooner may the rivers run backward and the course of the heavens change than any one soul that is united to Jesus Christ by faith and love can be severed from Him."

These were strange words to Woodruff. He only half understood and yet he could not forget them. He looked forward to meeting Daniel. Having dragged from the Captain the details of the wound he had snatched a hurried meal and then set out.

The night was dark and the Captain's directions

vague. Trees and bushes seemed to crouch in alarming postures. Were the enemy lying in wait? Fears crowded in on him. He felt alone and inadequate, and convinced that he had been sent on a mission not only doomed to fail but intended to fail. He was being used as a pawn in a vital game of chess, and pawns are often sacrificed carelessly.

This thought infuriated him and gave him fresh courage. He stumbled across the heath following the ill-made track by the light of his lantern. A dark shape loomed among the trees. That must be the house. It was in darkness. He felt at the door which gave at his touch. It had been left open. He went in and found Daniel lying at his feet. He knelt down and was relieved to find that the old man was still alive and that his wound had been cleaned. Who had done that? Where was this ward of his about whom Canting had talked? He was pondering this when he heard a noise outside. He tensed himself and his hand sought his sword.

The door was flung open and staff in hand Andrew charged in.

"Leave him, you've done enough harm. Defend yourself!" he cried.

Woodruff whipped his sword out, and gazed at the dark figure in some amazement. Behind another man entered.

"Listen ... " began the officer.

"Defend yourself," screamed Andrew who wielded his staff so furiously that Woodruff was driven back into a corner. In a flash Andrew bent down and snatched up Daniel's sword which he had known was lying beside its master.

"Fight, soldier. It's no man of seventy you have to deal with now," cried Andrew flinging the staff behind him. "Fight, you coward!" Andrew threw himself forward.

Again Lieutenant Woodruff attempted to call a truce, but his words were halted by the fury of Andrew's onslaught. The light from the one guttering lantern was bad, and it was well he was an expert swordsman, for had one of Andrew's lightning thrusts gone unparried his career would have ended there.

As it was he survived the assault, and though he realized that his opponent was a good swordsman, a glow of confidence surged through the officer as he realized he was a better.

Andrew was in a bad way. In his first wild fury all his aches and pains had been forgotten. He had rushed in to avenge the cowardly attack on Daniel, but as his lunge and thrusts clanged harmlessly against his adversary's steel, he felt his strength ebbing, and his head was aching so violently that it seemed it must burst. Peter Virley, staff in hand, perhaps sensing the way the battle was going, tried to come between the contestants.

"Stand back, Peter!" yelled Andrew. "This is my fight."

As Peter stood back he looked at the Lieutenant who had fought his way out of the shadows into the light of the lantern.

"This is not the man, Andrew. This is not the officer who came this afternoon," he shouted wildly.

Dimly Andrew heard the words, and as he understood them his sword dropped to his side. Woodruff checked his thrust. Peter seized Andrew's arm.

"This is not the man. He's younger and slimmer. Good sir," he said turning to the Lieutenant, "you must forgive my friend. His guardian was attacked and wounded this afternoon by an officer and he made the pardonable mistake of thinking that officer to be you." This was one of the longest speeches Peter had ever made and he sighed with exhaustion as he finished. Andrew stood there sullenly eyeing the Lieutenant.

"If it wasn't him, Peter, it was his companion. There's little difference." And he would have begun again in spite of his condition, had not Peter held his arm in a vice-like grip.

Woodruff, his sword at the ready, watched the men's two faces shrewdly. Years later when he was not a mere Lieutenant but a General, he was to be famous as a remarkable judge of character. He looked at the two as the light flickered on their faces, and he knew these were not the traitors he sought. He lowered his sword.

"I regret this gentleman was wounded. I am innocent of the deed," he said, nodding towards Daniel, "and may I assure you I am willing to do all I can to assist in his recovery. But it's no use crying over spilt milk. He must be moved to his bed, and the wound must be bandaged."

Peter, appreciating the agricultural proverb, hastened to help the Lieutenant as he made a move to lift Daniel. Andrew followed them dazedly. As the old man was placed on the bed, his eyes opened and he tried to speak.

"A .. Andrew," he began, but the effort was too much and he relapsed back into unconsciousness.

7

ANDREW sank down on a chair exhausted. Peter stood beside him. Woodruff thought fast. If he trusted to his judgment these two might prove useful friends, but one doubt remained. The Captain's snuff-box. Two things were certain. It had been stolen from Captain Canting by the highwayman and the Captain had found it in the school desk of Daniel's cottage. Andrew must produce a satisfactory answer to that problem before he could be trusted. A pang of pity went through the Lieutenant as he looked at Andrew, his head buried in his hands and obviously faint from fatigue and distress, but he put it to one side. He must get the information he required, and he must get it quickly.

"Daniel Foot is suspected of being a traitor," he began brusquely, watching Andrew closely.

Andrew looked up with amazement on his face, but said nothing.

"Daniel Foot was no traitor," said Peter slowly.

"I do not say he was. I merely say he's suspected of being one. There is evidence against him," replied the Lieutenant.

"Evidence? What evidence?" asked Andrew, sitting up straight.

"Captain Canting and I have been sent to Lindfield to investigate Jacobite gun-running which has been carried on on a large scale. There is little doubt that the operations are controlled from here." Remembering his adventure in the quarry Andrew could not help giving a start of excitement at hearing this, a start which was duly noted by the observant Lieutenant.

"On our journey here," he continued, "our coach was stopped by a highwayman. He took from us what few valuables we had including a snuff-box from Captain Canting, but it seemed to me that his real interest lay not in these valuables but in certain documents we were carrying, containing details of our mission, which he also took; this morning Captain Canting received an unsigned note which directed him to search in the desk in Daniel Foot's house. This he did and it was while he was doing this that his unfortunate encounter with the old man took place."

"'Tis a strange soldier that attacks an old man of seventy," growled Peter.

"What did he find in the desk?" asked Andrew tensely.

"He found his snuff-box," said Lieutenant Woodruff.

"His snuff-box, the one he had stolen by the highwayman?" cried Andrew in what sounded to the Lieutenant like genuine amazement.

"The very same!"

"But how did it get there?"

"That was what I wanted to ask you."

"Me? How should I know? You don't think I am anything to do with your highwayman and your Jacobites, do you?"

"No, I don't, but I must make sure. How did it get there?" The Lieutenant was calm but persistent.

"I don't know, I don't know, I tell you," cried Andrew burying his head in his hands again.

Peter stepped forward. "The boy's had enough. Leave your questions to the morning."

"I'm sorry. The issue may be vital, and an hour lost now may affect greater events than you dream of." So resolute did the Lieutenant sound that Peter stepped reluctantly back. Lieutenant Woodruff returned to his interrogation.

"Had you any visitors yesterday?"

"I don't think so," began Andrew wearily. The events of yesterday seemed so far away. "Oh, yes. Carson came but he couldn't have anything to do with the snuff-box." But even as he spoke he remembered the strange circumstances of his friend's visit.

"Carson?" said the Lieutenant sharply. "Who is he?"

Andrew explained, stressing his long-standing friendship with Sir Humphrey's son. Woodruff listened carefully.

"And was he the only visitor?"

"Yes, as far as I...." Then Andrew gave a sudden cry. He had forgotten the intruder of last night. *He* could have done it. That would explain why he had taken nothing. He had come to *bring* something! Andrew told the story of the previous night. As Woodruff heard it some suspicions crept into his mind. The story and explanation seemed too convenient, too neat—and why had Andrew not thought of it before? Where was Andrew's proof? He could not know that Andrew's failure to remember the coming of the intruder was due to the dramatic events of the day and to his own exhaustion. But now Andrew's mind cleared as he began to see a connecting link in the train of events. At any rate the fact of the intruder's coming pointed to Carson's innocence in the matter.

"Have you any proof of your story?" asked Woodruff.

"Daniel will confirm it, and," said Andrew smiling ruefully, "feel the back of my head."

The Lieutenant did so. Certainly Andrew had suffered recently from a savage blow.

"Your wound speaks eloquently for you. I take your word, and now we must consider our plans. You realize that our Jacobite friends are making a determined effort to see that the trail we are following leads to you."

"Yes, I see that, but why? You must find out that we are innocent in the end."

"In the end, aye, but by then it would be too late. We know—and this is about all we do know, thanks to the work of Nicholas Mole—that the Jacobites' work here finishes on Friday. My guess is that on Friday from somewhere in this region arms and ammunition in large quantities will start a journey and that they will find their way shortly into the houses of Jacobite sympathizers all over the country—and there are many. That could mean civil war, and civil war is an ugly thing."

Peter and Andrew watched the Lieutenant's face as he put the position before them. The lantern light was smoky and dim, but it showed them clearly enough that he was honest and serious.

"I need your help," said Woodruff. "Will you give it?"

There was a silence. Peter thought of his farm—his life. He couldn't leave that. What help would be needed? Andrew thought of his discovery in the quarry. Surely he had found the key to the matter. But, and this nagging thought remained; what about Carson? Would he be betraying his best friend?

And then Woodruff had a surprise.

"I know what Daniel would do now," said Andrew looking at the still figure on the bed.

"And so do I," said Peter quietly. He turned to the Lieutenant and said, "We are going to ask for help from One Who knows the answer to all our difficulties."

Peter and Andrew then knelt down at Daniel's bedside. First Peter prayed and then Andrew. Their prayers were not long, but simple and to the point. They prayed for

Daniel, and for guidance about what to do. Woodruff had never thought before of praying as anything but one of the ingredients of a church service. What struck him most as he stood looking in some astonishment at the two friends on their knees was the fact that their prayers seemed to be addressed to a friend, to someone they knew well. Forty-eight hours ago he would have laughed heartily at them, but Woodruff had changed in forty-eight hours and he felt no inclination to laugh. Though he did not admit it, he experienced a strange sense of security as these two prayed so confidently to God. "At least it can't do any harm," he thought to himself.

The two rose.

"We must get a doctor for Daniel," said Peter. "There's no doctor in Lindfield, but Sir Humphrey will send a messenger to Ditchling for old Doctor Nicol, a friend of his."

"I'll go," said Andrew.

"No, Andrew," said Peter. "I'll go. Daniel will not need to wait long for his doctor."

"Thank you," replied the Lieutenant. "I think your help may well be needed."

With a brief word of farewell Peter slipped out into the night.

"And now," said Woodruff, not unkindly, "I think you have something more to tell me."

"I have," said Andrew, "but how did you know?"

"You betrayed yourself, Andrew, when I mentioned the gun-running being carried on near Lindfield. You can help me there?"

"Yes, I can, and I was about to do so." Andrew told his story as accurately as he could. Woodruff's eyes sparkled with delight as he heard of Andrew's discovery in the cave of the quarry. Surely the game was his now! A pawn can checkmate a king.

"When did you leave the quarry?" asked the Lieutenant as Andrew finished his account.

"About four hours ago."

"Then, unless they have worked fast those coffins will still be there. And it won't be long before I am there too, to put a few nails in their coffins. Now Andrew you must give me as clear a picture as possible of this quarrry and the way there."

Andrew would have liked very much to accompany him there, for his feelings towards the Lieutenant had undergone a considerable change in the last hour, but that could not be, so he contented himself with giving as clear and helpful instructions as he could.

Woodruff noted everything carefully, and then smiled at Andrew. "You've played your part in the first act. The stage is mine now, but don't forget there's still Act Two. Your orders are to stay with Daniel and get in as much sleep as you can. Don't leave him till he is being properly tended. I'm looking forward to meeting him when he's fit and well. When the sawbones arrives get him to instruct some woman in how to nurse him. Do you know anyone who would help?"

"Yes, Nancy Goodwin who takes in our washing will come. She's done it before."

"Good. And that'll leave you free for action, I'll be back here by nine in the morning. If I'm not I give you full permission to come and rescue me." The Lieutenant smiled at his own little joke. "Farewell, Andrew. Wish me God speed." And then he was gone.

Andrew lay on some sacking by Daniel's bed and, before Woodruff was twenty yards from the house, Andrew was asleep.

At the same time, Peter Virley was returning to his farm well satisfied with his night's work. He had arrived at Sir Humphrey's and had seen to his satisfaction some lights still burning. He had not looked forward to the task of waking a sleeping household. To his surprise, his tap on the door brought an almost immediate response. The door was opened on to a hall bright with candlelight. While Peter blinked a sharp voice said "Well?"

Peter saw a tall well-dressed man with steely eyes looking at him. They were not friendly.

"I want to speak to Sir Humphrey," said Peter.

"He is in bed. But if it is urgent I shall see he is given any message."

Peter gave his message slightly uneasily. As he finished a smile played round the face of the listener.

"I think I can help you without disturbing Sir Humphrey or even good Doctor Nicol of Ditchling. I am Brookestone, Sir Humphrey's lawyer and friend, and by great good fortune a doctor friend of mine is lodging this night in Lindfield. I'll send a messenger for him at once. Excuse me while I pen a note of explanation."

The lawyer's sudden friendliness and offers of assistance had rather bewildered Peter, but it seemed to him as he stood there in the doorway that if indeed there was a doctor in Lindfield then Daniel would get the help he needed more quickly and that was all that mattered. The lawyer soon reappeared with the note, which he handed to a burly and roughly dressed servant who came on the scene as if by magic. After a few words spoken so quietly that Peter did not catch them the servant slipped out of the door.

The lawyer came across towards Peter.

"Your friend will soon have the help he needs. Daniel Foot, I believe you said. I have heard many excellent things about him."

"Yes, he's been a good friend to me," said Peter.

"Well, now is our chance to repay some of his kindness to others."

"You are very good, sir."

"No, do not thank me. My reward will be to hear that all goes well with Daniel Foot. Now the hour is late and I must retire. Good night, sir." And the great door closed leaving Peter in the darkness. On the other side of the door Brookestone stood still for a moment as if deep in thought. A strangely satisfied look came over his face.

Meanwhile the lawyer's messenger reached Walstead Cottage. His knocking brought the owner of the house angrily to the door. He was little mollified when he found it was the gentleman for whom he was providing lodging for a few nights that was required. However, he reflected that he was being well paid and grumblingly went to wake his lodger.

Soon a short swarthy man appeared in the doorway. His expression was sleepy. The messenger thrust the note at him, and waited hopefully, but in vain. As the doctor read the note his expression tautened, bushy eyebrows met over two eyes that were now anything but sleepy. The messenger stepped back involuntarily and then turned away, muttering, "These foreigners. And not a wink o' sleep yet tonight."

The messenger returned towards the Hall. Peter was back at his beloved farm, Lieutenant Woodruff had reached the spinney, and was crashing through the undergrowth towards the quarry, and in his cottage Daniel was stirring.

8

Some hours later Andrew groaned as he turned over. A twinge of pain made him open his eyes. Where was he?

"Good morning, Andrew," said a voice that Andrew knew well.

"Daniel!" cried Andrew, springing up. "Thank God! You're alive!" He seized Daniel's white but sinewy hands. "What happened, Daniel?" Daniel smiled, "I'll tell you when we've both eaten."

Before long Andrew produced some steaming oats and while they both enjoyed the cheering warmth of the food they told one another the story of yesterday. Daniel agreed with Andrew about the probable purpose of the night intruder.

"But what I can't understand is why anyone should want to involve us."

"It's a matter of killing two birds with one stone, Andrew," replied Daniel. "You've learnt that if the plot is not discovered by Friday then the plotters will have attained their object. Thus a false trail might give them more time."

"That's one bird, but what's the other?"

"I'm the other bird. You see, I know too much."

"You? Well, why didn't you tell me?" Andrew sounded aggrieved.

"I had made a promise, Andrew, and that promise still

binds me, but there is much I have to tell you. I think that after yesterday I owe it to you, and I have a feeling I may not have many more opportunities."

"But you're recovering. Doctor Nicol will be here soon. Why do you say not many more opportunities?"

A faint smile creased Daniel's white face.

"It is only a feeling, Andrew. Now are you in the mood for a history lesson?" Without waiting for an answer Daniel embarked on the lesson.

"My great-great-grandfather was a Frenchman. His name was Daniel de Pied. He lived in a village not far from La Rochelle."

"That was the Huguenot town, wasn't it?"

"Yes, that was the stronghold of French Protestantism, which had for many years resisted the attacks and wiles of the Catholic party. They were hard days. If a Huguenot were captured a quick death was the best he could hope for. The Duke of Guise was determined to root out what he considered was heresy from France, and he favoured any means which furthered his ends. This persecution came to a head in the dreadful cruelty of August 24th, 1572, the Feast of St. Bartholomew. My great-great-grandfather was a carpenter, and he lived in a small house with his wife and nine-year-old son in the main street of the village. On the afternoon of the 23rd, Pierre, his son, noticed a strange thing. A white cross had been chalked over the doorway of the house. He pointed this out to his mother, but she, thinking it was some boyish game, paid little attention. However, she did mention it casually to her husband when he returned and he took it more seriously. He went out and looked at the chalk cross and then discovered that several other houses in the street were similarly marked—they were all houses of Huguenots. The sufferings of the past had made Daniel alert to danger.

"Immediately he called on his Huguenot friends and

told them of his suspicions. Some merely smiled in disbelief, but one, a butcher, supported him and he agreed that in case of emergencies he would have his two wagons waiting behind his shop ready to depart for La Rochelle.

"That night Daniel did not go to bed. He waited. Not long after midnight he heard unusual noises and opening the door slightly, he looked out. A body of soldiers was standing in the street about thirty yards away. This was enough for Daniel. He roused his wife and son and told them to go to the butcher's and get a place in the wagon. He told them he would join them later. Even as they escaped by the back way a huge axe descended on the front door. Another blow and the door crashed in. Grim-faced soldiers poured in. Shrieks up and down the street told the story of their brutal work.

"Daniel met them with his sword. The axeman fell back never to ply an axe again, but others pressed forward, murder in their eyes and hands. And so Daniel died."

"What about his wife and child?" asked Andrew eagerly.

"Some water, Andrew, please. I feel faint."

Andrew hastened for a mug of water, which Daniel sipped thankfully.

"Thank you. Yes, Daniel's wife and child escaped to La Rochelle. When she heard for certain that her husband was dead, she decided with many other Huguenots to go to a country where there was freedom to read the Bible and worship as they pleased. When they arrived in England Denise became cook—and I'm told there was never a cook like her—with a family called Dale." Andrew gave a start. At last he was hearing what he had always longed to hear—the tale of his family. "Pierre grew up to be a carpenter on the estate. He changed his name to Foot and married an English girl. Pierre's son Daniel and his son Peter likewise served the Dales. But the Civil War brought tragedy. Your grandfather fought bravely on the Parliamentary side and was killed at Naseby at the moment of triumph. My father was killed fighting beside him. Thus your father, then eight years old, was left as head of the family, and he and I being of much the same age became close friends. Then came the restoration of Charles 11. In spite of promises many who had fought on the Parliamentary side were persecuted, and one day in 1661 when we were returning from business in London we found Kineton House in ruins. It had been burnt to the ground by some drunken young Royalist sympathizers returning from a party. There was no redress. Your father had not enough money to build again and so he sold the estate and we lived in lodgings in London. Your father became silent and often morose, but never bitter. What saved him, I think, was his love of the Bible. He earned some money teaching, which with the money your father had from the sale of the estate was enough for our needs.

"Then came the reign of James II, a Roman Catholic, and one who meant to impose Romanism on Protestant England. All that your father and I believed in was at stake once again. Your father hated strife, but he hated the oppression of the Catholics more. When news reached London of Monmouth's landing and rising in the West, your father left immediately to join the rebels. Our journey was difficult, but we succeeded in joining Monmouth's forces at Bridgewater. It was a strange army. The peasants of the West had joined him enthusiastically, but the gentry and squires had not. There were few competent officers, and just as serious was the shortage of arms. Scythes, bludgeons, and pitchforks were the main weapons. We had some muskets but little enough ammunition for them.

"I remember that Sunday, July 5th, as clearly as if it were yesterday. Bridgewater was afire for King Monmouth, as he had been proclaimed. There was no one who did not wear his emblem, a green sprig in their hats. Then came the news that James' army had pitched their tents on the plain of Sedgemoor, not three miles away, and with that news came the rain—driving, drenching rain that made every road a river and every stream a torrent.

"That evening Monmouth's spies reported much drinking and merry-making among the royal force, and he decided to make a surprise attack that night. Your father was in charge of thirty footsoldiers on Monmouth's right and I was with him. We were both armed with muskets and swords. We marched all that night. The moor was almost a marsh, and wet mists swirled low. However the moon was full and we made good time. Two muddy, deep streams gave us some trouble, and then just as we were crossing the second someone fired a musket. One of the royal sentries heard the report and the alarm was raised."

"So the whole plan of a surprise attack failed?" said Andrew.

"Yes, and with it went Monmouth's hopes. He gave the order to charge, but he made another mistake. There was yet another stream to cross—one of which he had taken no account. Our men floundered in as the first volley of the royal musketry burst among us. Your father led us across the stream—those that weren't drowned—but there was no chance against the well-drilled cavalry of the Royal Horse Guards. The peasants fought like heroes, many with only their scythes; some had muskets and when ammunition ran out, as it soon did, they used the butt ends as clubs, but it was hopeless. There was no reply to the withering fire from the Horse Guards. In less than half-an-hour the battle was lost and Monmouth's army scattered.

"Your father's left arm had been shattered by a musket

shot, but he had fought to the last, encouraging his men. When all was lost we slipped away in the mist, as the royal army sought to round up Monmouth's supporters. Sorry was the fate of those who were captured."

"They were tried by Judge Jeffreys, weren't they?"

"Tried! There was no trial. It was the lowest level to which English justice has ever sunk. But we escaped. Your father and I spent the night in a ditch not twenty yards from the enemy. I shall never forget your father's courage and faith during those hours. He was painfully wounded, but he never complained of that. The first thing we did as we lay there was to pray. Your father prayed two things. First that England might have a Protestant King, and second that the soldiers might not find us.

"'They won't find us now,' your father said, as soon as he had finished praying, and they didn't. At dawn they moved away still hunting for the remnants of the army, and we crawled from our ditch and after a difficult day we found shelter in the house of a brave farmer near Bridge-water."

"Didn't they search the house?" asked Andrew.

"That they did, but they didn't find us—we were in an attic to which the only entrance was through the chimney, and that was no pleasant task. Our food was brought up by the bonny daughter of the farmer. But to bring this tedious history to an end, six weeks later your father married her. She was your mother."

Andrew stared at Daniel as he sank back on the pillow exhausted by the effort he had made. There had been nothing tedious to Andrew about this history lesson. Questions thronged Andrew's brain.

"But why, why didn't you tell me this before?" he cried. For most of his life Andrew had asked questions about his parents, but Daniel had always remained silent.

"Because of a promise I made to your father shortly before he died. After Sedgemoor he never recovered his health, and the blow of losing his wife shortly after you were born made him more taciturn and gloomy than before. Much of his misfortune he put down to the Civil Wars and high religious feeling which had torn England apart, and his great wish was that you should be spared what he had gone through.

"He lived to see his first prayer in that Sedgemoor ditch answered as the second had been. A Protestant king again ruled England and the Bible again was an open book. His last prayer for you was that you should serve the same Heavenly Master, the Lord Jesus Christ; but the past, the bitter past for him, should be forgotten."

"But you cannot wipe out the past. That past is part of me."

"I think now you're right, Andrew. That past is part of you. Perhaps that is why you're fighting for the same cause that your father did."

"I wish . . ." began Andrew, but he was interrupted by a sharp rap on the door. "Ah, that will be Doctor Nicol from Ditchling. He must have ridden hard." He hurried to the door and opened it, and then stepped back in surprise, for instead of the friendly red face of Doctor Nicol, the dark face of a stranger confronted him. He was arrayed in a black cloak and carried a black bag. The stranger smiled.

"This is the house of Daniel Foot?" he queried.

"Yes," replied Andrew, a tinge of suspicion in his voice.

"I am Doctor Carter," said the stranger briskly. "I am lodging in Lindfield for a few nights and I have just received a message from the Hall to say that Daniel Foot has suffered an injury to his leg."

"Yes," said Andrew stepping back from the threshold. "He's lying in here. Come in." His suspicions had vanished when he heard that a message from the Hall had brought about the arrival of the Doctor. If Sir Humphrey had sent him, then he must be all right.

They found Daniel lying back with his eyes closed. The effort of telling his story to Andrew had been a great one. Andrew ran to him. "Daniel," he said softly. "Here's the Doctor."

Daniel's eyelids flickered a moment and he smiled faintly but said nothing.

Doctor Carter knelt down and examined the wound. He turned to Andrew.

"Bring me some water," he rapped out in a voice that commanded obedience. Andrew brought water.

"How is he?" he asked.

"Poisoning has set in," snapped Doctor Carter. "The wound has not been cleaned properly." Andrew said nothing. He had done his best and the wound had seemed clean.

The Doctor stood up. "Some water in a cup, quickly," he ordered. When Andrew had brought it, Doctor Carter opened his black bag and pulled out a phial containing a white powder. He tipped the powder into the water.

"He must drink this at once," he said. "It's the only way to combat the poison. I fear we may be too late already. I suggest you make him drink it." Doctor Carter handed the cup to Andrew, who took it reluctantly. There was something about Doctor Carter he distrusted, but he was unable to give himself any good reason. Doctor Carter saw him hesitate.

"Hurry," he said. "Do you not want to save his life?" It was the way he talked, Andrew decided. His preciseness suggested a foreigner rather than an Englishman.

"Why don't you give it to him?" asked Andrew.

"You foolish boy!" cried the Doctor. "Only because he knows you and will feel happier if you give it to him.

Hurry! Every second is precious." Andrew turned to Daniel.

"Daniel, can you hear me?" he said. The old man nodded faintly. "The Doctor wants you to drink this. Can you do it?" asked Andrew.

"He must do it," said Doctor Carter urgently. Again Daniel nodded. Andrew put the cup to the old man's lips and slowly he sipped it down till the cup was empty.

"Good," said the Doctor. "We may save him. He will sleep now and will awake refreshed." He closed his bag. Andrew watched him silently.

"I will come back this afternoon. The old man will be all right till then."

"Where are you staying, in case he needs you before then?"

"He will not need me before then," replied Doctor Carter with some asperity in his voice. He had reached the door.

"Good-bye, young man," he said.

"Good-bye," said Andrew dully. He watched the black-cloaked doctor hurry away. "More like a priest's cloak than a doctor's," he thought idly to himself. He went back to look at Daniel, who was now breathing more heavily. Sweat glistened on his white forehead. Andrew felt miserable and uncertain. He paced up and down the room trying to compose his jumbled thoughts. How was Lieutenant Woodruff faring at the quarry? He should be back before long. What if he didn't come back? Just then Daniel murmured something. Andrew hurried to kneel beside him.

"I'm here. It's Andrew," he said.

Daniel opened his eyes and spoke clearly and slowly.

"I am dying, Andrew." He ignored Andrew's attempted denials. "No, Andrew, do not worry or grieve. Jesus Who shed His blood to save me waits to take me to the eternal home, and that is where I long to go." He placed his cold hand on Andrew's. "God bless you, Andrew. May Jesus our Saviour give you His love and courage day by day and may you fight for Him till we meet again." Daniel's head dropped back to the pillow.

"Daniel!" cried Andrew, but Daniel lay still. A faithful warrior had fought his last battle.

9

LIEUTENANT Woodruff stumbled and slithered as he crossed the fields towards the spinney. He did without his lantern. The moon shone palely through the clouds, and the Lieutenant could not afford to be seen. Andrew's directions had been good, and it was not long before he saw the outline of the larches against the sky.

"Good for Andrew!" he thought, and his heart warmed towards the young man who a few hours before had tried to kill him. He paused to decide on the best line of approach, and as he did so a sound of voices was borne to him on the light spring breeze. Woodruff froze and listened. Voices in the spinney! So the plotters were resuming the work that Andrew had interrupted. Lieutenant Woodruff knew why. Time was short for them. The arms must be on their way to their destinations within twenty-four hours. But time was short for him too. He had, he was certain, gone a long way towards unravelling the plot, but he knew he must find out exactly where the arms were, and just as important he must find the master-mind behind the plot. The pawn must take the queen, but the queen was a powerful piece, and Lieutenant Woodruff had no illusions about the difficulties of his task.

As he drew nearer the spinney the occasional gleam of a lantern through the trees confirmed his suspicions about the activities in the quarry. Reaching the spinney he allowed himself to be guided by the voices. The briars ripped at his coat and branches stung his face, but soon he was overlooking the quarry at the opposite end from the cave. His heart thumped violently with excitement. There in the lurid light of three lanterns were six men at work loading three wagons which stood on the shallow slope to the quarry.

Sinking down behind a bush, the Lieutenant watched fascinated. They seemed to have no guard or no thought that they might be watched. They complained and swore loudly as they manoeuvred their awkward burdens out of the cave and across the stepping-stones to the wagons, which were already piled high with the coffins, the contents of which were doubtless intended to help drive Queen Anne from the throne.

Woodruff had already decided what he must do. To attack now would be useless. He might kill one or two with his pistol, though the sword was the weapon he preferred, but there were six of them and two at least he could see were armed with pistols. It was probable they were better shots than he. No, his plan of action must be to follow the wagons and find out exactly where they went and what happened to the coffins. They would remain in Lindfield at least till the next day, unless there had been a change of plan, and anyway the plotters could not possibly take these wagons piled high with coffins on the highways in the daytime. How were they going to be distributed? As soon as he knew the answer to that he was confident that a message to a troop of the Earl of Howell's Dragons stationed at Reigate would bring him enough help to make sure the arms never reached their destinations.

The young officer watched the men, closely memorizing their faces and clothes as best he could in the muddy light. Their voices suggested to him that some were Londoners, and one of them seemed to be called Joe.

Suddenly the strident tones of their voices were hushed.

Woodruff ducked back behind the bush. Had they seen him? The silence, uncanny to the officer, continued. They could not have seen him, he reassured himself. He peered cautiously round his bush. The men were still heaving the coffins out of the cave and across the marsh, but they were working in absolute silence. What had caused the change? Even when one of the men slipped and went up to the thigh in the marsh—an event which would have called forth a volley of oaths before—there was silence.

Woodruff's keen eyes scanned the scene and found the answer. A seventh figure had appeared. There on a mound beyond the carts stood a dark figure, outside the flicker of the lanterns and little more than a silhouette against the moonlit sky. With a thrill in his heart he realized that this was not just another labourer in the pay of the plotters; this was someone whose mere presence called forth instant respect. Perhaps this was the leader. In vain did he strain his eyes to tear some details from that still black silhouette. The darkness defeated him. From the angle of his vantage point he even found it hard to estimate whether the man was short or tall, though he guessed that the latter was the truer judgment.

He was sorely tempted to throw caution to the winds, creep round the quarry and then hurl himself at the black figure. With one thrust of his sword the whole plot might be ripped asunder. But the hazard was too great. His life was precious because of the information he hoped to gain; if he died, and there seemed little prospect of a safe return from such a venture, the plot might be safely carried through without a leader. And then he could not be sure that the still figure standing forty yards from him was indeed the master plotter. He decided he must play a waiting game. He must know what happened to those coffins. If only the seventh man would step into the light of the lanterns!

Each wagon was now well loaded, and the man called Joe went forward and spoke quietly to the black statue. There must have been a reply, but Woodruff, leaning perilously beyond his shelter, could see or hear nothing. Joe waved his arm and four men gathered round the rear of the wagons while Joe and another coaxed the horses forward. The horses strained and the men behind heaved. With a great squelch the wagons lurched out of their sodden rut and slowly moved up the incline towards the fields. The dark figure, still motionless, watched this operation, and then to Woodruff's disappointment turned and disappeared into the sombre shadows of the spinney.

The Lieutenant left his hiding-place and followed the swaying lanterns, making the best use he could of cover. Through the spinney it was not difficult, but when the wagons reached the fields he heard Joe give an order and the three lanterns went out.

The wagons trundled across the fields in the direction of Lindfield. Woodruff was faced with the alternatives of either following straight across the field—in which case he would need to drop at least a hundred yards behind— or of keeping considerably closer by using the shadow of the hedges as cover. There was an element of risk about the latter course, but Woodruff was aware of his lack of local knowledge and was determined that his quarry must not get too far ahead, so without hesitation he entrusted himself to the protection of the hedges.

He felt uncomfortably naked as he darted along not forty yards from the wagons, for the moon slid from behind a cloud and cast its silver light over the scene. But Joe and his men did not seem disposed to look around. They grumbled as they plodded on, but in tones more subdued than they had used previously.

Joe himself was distinctly worried. He had not had the

courage to tell the Master of his unsuccessful brush with Andrew earlier that night, though he had had some difficulty in explaining to the Master why he and Jesse had managed to carry so few coffins during the early part of the night. Now he was almost hoping that the unexpected intruder would appear again, so that he might have a chance to level the scores and ensure that the secret did not leak out. Thus Joe was on the alert.

Woodruff, famed in London for his immaculate appearance, was anything but immaculate now. His shiny boots were bedaubed by the mud of the ditches along which he half crawled and half ran. His clothes were torn and soiled and his wig was wispy and ragged. For some time he was successful in keeping close to his quarry, but then came disaster. With a sudden rustle a disturbed jay—blue-winged Judas indeed!—rose chackering from the hedge beside him. He froze instantly.

Joe looked round.

"What was that, Jesse?" he growled.

"Only a jay," came the reply.

"Ah, but what made him rise? It wasn't us. We are well past the spot."

"A fox then."

"Or something just as cunning maybe." Joe stared at the dark hedge forty yards away. "Stop the wagons and follow me," he ordered. Quickly he told them what he suspected and in a broad line they advanced slowly towards the hedge.

Woodruff thought desperately. He slipped his pistol out of his holster. It had been primed before he had set out, and he pulled back the cocking piece with his thumb. The men came slowly on. And then Woodruff made a mistake. When the men were twenty yards away he shouted "Halt, or I fire!"

Had he but known it he was still invisible to the men,

and Joe himself was just coming to the conclusion that they were on a wild goose chase—a conclusion which his five comrades had arrived at from the beginning.

"Halt, or I fire!"

The men halted and looked to Joe. Joe peered at the hedge and caught the glint of the polished barrel in the moonlight.

Joe was no coward. He glanced round at his men. Three had swords. They had no firearms. He had discarded his musket in disgust.

"Charge," he shouted, and sword in hand he dashed forward. The others hesitated and then rushed forward, reflecting perhaps that the pistol would be aimed at Joe. It was, but Woodruff shot too soon and his hand was not steady enough. The bullet passed close to Joe but it passed. Woodruff wrenched at his sword, and was just in time to parry a furious lunge from Joe. But the odds were hopeless. As he repelled Joe's attacks two other blades glinted cruelly in the moonlight. There was no retreat. He flung himself on Joe and beat the sword from his hand but even as he did so a stunning blow from behind dealt by a club of Jesse's knocked him forward half senseless on to the field. Joe flung himself on the body, gripping the arm in which Woodruff held his sword.

"Finish him off," said Joe, panting, as he held the half-stunned officer on the ground. Woodruff struggled, but he knew it was in vain and in that moment there flashed into his mind the action of Andrew and Peter when confronted with a difficulty. They had prayed, and at that moment Woodruff prayed his first prayer. "O God, save me."

"Through his heart, Harry," growled Joe, shifting to allow the swordsman to see his target. Harry raised his sword, and then dropped it again irresolutely.

"I can't kill him like that," he said.

"Obey orders," roared Joe who was desperately engaged in pinioning the struggling Lieutenant.

Harry did not reply but stepped back.

"Hand me my sword then, you lily-livered dog."

Harry spoke again.

"No, Joe, not murder. Our job is to move them coffins. What's in 'em I don't guess. I'll obey your orders about moving them coffins, but murder, no."

The murmur of approval from the other four convinced Joe that he was alone. He thought quickly, realizing the importance of re-establishing his leadership. "We'll take him prisoner," he said, rising. Woodruff rose unsteadily to his feet. Escape he knew was impossible.

"He's a redcoat," said Jesse looking at the tattered remains of Woodruff's uniform.

"So he is," said Joe unpleasantly. "And that red coat of his will be useful. Have it off him." Joe and Jesse ripped it off and then Joe started tearing it up.

"Round his eyes," he said, giving a strip to Jesse. With another strip Joe gagged his prisoner with unnecessary viciousness and then securely bound his wrists behind his back with the remains of Woodruff's coat.

"You carry on with the wagons," he ordered. "Jesse knows what to do with them. I'll join you when I've dealt with our fine young officer." Joe himself had served in the Army on the Continent some years before. He had not been a success as a soldier; his blustering ways and inability to obey commands often gaining him the harsh punishments then in force in the Army. Shortly before Blenheim he deserted, and returned to England carrying with him a deep hatred of the Army and especially of its officers. That was probably why Woodruff had such a miserable walk to captivity. Joe pushed him roughly along. Woodruff soon gave up any hope of keeping his bearings. He stumbled blindly on with despair in his heart. His self-confidence had been shattered at one blow. Just as he was feeling he could go no further a rough push from Joe sent him sprawling forward on to some wooden boards. He heard a door closed and locked behind him. He lay there miserably trying to release his bonds, but before he had any success he heard the door opened again.

"Get up," ordered Joe roughly. "This way."

The Lieutenant soon felt a stone corridor ringing beneath his feet and then he was forced upstairs. The stairs were wooden. He counted carefully, thirty steps. At the top, a shove from Joe propelled him along a corridor.

"In here," said Joe seizing him by the arm and pushing him through a doorway. He heard the heavy door slammed and locked behind him.

He stood listening as Joe's footsteps rang hollowly down the corridor. He must try to think clearly. There was so little time. He must get in touch with Andrew. The first thing obviously was to free himself from his bonds, and after exploring the possibilities of the room, he set about it.

It was some hours before Andrew was able to turn his mind to the problem of the non-appearance of Woodruff. At first his grief at the death of Daniel had numbed all other thoughts, but that morning he had prayed, and when he rose from his knees the ache of grief was almost displaced by a sense of peace and confidence. Daniel, he knew, had gone where he longed to go and he remembered his old friend's last prayer for him—"May Jesus, our Saviour, give you His love and courage every day." Courage. Andrew knew he would need it now.

He then hurried off to the Vicar, who was much saddened by his news. The Rev. Thomas Bysshe lived in an age of lukewarm faith, and many a time had sought and found encouragement and advice from Daniel, whose burning zeal for his Master had never grown cold. He was horrified to hear of the sword wound and urged Andrew to report it at once to Sir Humphrey, the local Justice of the Peace, but this Andrew seemed reluctant to do. The Vicar then offered that Andrew should stay with him at the Vicarage, and was secretly most thankful when he refused, for there was not a bed in the place save his own.

When the arrangements for the burial were complete Andrew hurried to tell Peter, who also offered accommodation. This time Andrew accepted. Peter was busy unloading a wagon of hay on to a roadside stack, which was to be collected that day for carriage to London.

Hearing of Daniel's death made Peter more uncommunicative than ever. It was only when Andrew told him of his suspicions about the doctor that Peter was persuaded to relate the story of his visit to Steadwell Hall. Andrew's interest grew when he discovered it was not Sir Humphrey whom Peter had seen; his eager questions dragged from the farmer a fairly accurate description of the man who had opened the door to him. Andrew's eyes gleamed.

"That must have been Talbot Brookestone, the lawyer," he mused out loud. "I wonder why he was burning the midnight oil? And not only he—his servants as well." Peter offered no helpful answer. He was busy with his pitchfork, deftly and effortlessly shaping his stack.

"I'm interested in that lawyer," said Andrew to Peter as he slid down from the stack. "It is since he tutored Carson that Carson has become so strange. I must find out more about him." Peter hardly appeared to hear as he ran his eyes critically round the lines of the stack. Another thought occurred to Andrew. "And what about the Lieutenant? He was due back an hour ago."

Peter focused his mind on the problem. After some discussion they agreed that Peter should go straight to the quarry while Andrew would call at the Hall, inform them of Daniel's death, explain why he would not be able to tutor Sophia, and then hurry to join Peter at the quarry.

As Andrew approached the Hall he suddenly stopped and stared up at the gaunt old building. Something caught his eye. He stared a moment and then marched up to the door with a purposeful air.

When he had been ushered inside, he asked to see Sir Humphrey.

Sir Humphrey was sitting in his study. His smile of welcome changed as he learnt of Daniel's death, but not of its circumstances.

"My dear boy," he said, "I am sorry. I respected Daniel Foot greatly, very greatly. Well, you won't want to do any school-mastering today. I'll tell Sophia she will be free. Now, tell me, is there anything I can do to help?"

"Well, sir," replied Andrew, "if you don't mind, I'd rather carry on the lessons as usual today."

10

SOPHIA showed great sympathy when she heard Andrew's news. She had been fond of Daniel, but it was not long before they were discussing another subject. Playing on Sophia's dislike of Talbot Brookestone, Andrew told her that he must know where his rooms were, and added that he hoped as a result of his investigations that he would find out what was wrong with Carson. Much intrigued, Sophia gave him a clear and detailed description of the Hall. Andrew was particularly interested to discover in which wing the lawyer had his suite. Sophia could tell him nothing about any doctor friend that Brookestone might have, but Andrew was hardly surprised at this.

When he told her that he wanted to investigate that wing of the house while the household would be dining, the girl was most anxious to accompany him. It was only by promising to give her a full account of what happened that he managed to dissuade her, and even then she became very sulky and emphatically refused to do any Latin at all for the hour that remained before dinner. Strangely enough it was while she was pouting and scowling that Andrew noticed for the first time that she was beautiful, but this thought was quickly pushed aside. There was urgent work to be done. He prayed silently as the minutes crawled by.

"Will they all be at dinner now?" he asked at length. Sophia considered.

"It will be safer to wait a few more minutes," she said coldly.

Andrew stood by the door with ill-concealed impatience. Action he did not mind, but waiting was hard to bear. A few minutes passed. With a brief wave Andrew slipped out of the door. To his relief the hall was empty. Now for Sophia's instructions. Up the main stairs, good, no-one around, along the corridor that led to the East wing, where Talbot Brookestone's apartments were situated. Now where was the staircase to the servants' quarters above? He counted three doors along. No staircase. As he paused irresolutely he heard voices behind him. Two men were coming up the main staircase. Standing in the shadow of the doorway Andrew waited anxiously to hear which way they would turn. The voices grew louder. They were coming this way. To bluff it out or to hide? Andrew's mind worked fast. He chose the latter course. He could not risk being seen. He opened the door behind him and slipped quietly in. With a thrill of horror he realized that he had chosen Talbot Brookestone's study as a refuge. He had little time for further reflection. The voices came from just outside the door. The wooden latch moved. They were coming in. It was fortunate for Andrew that so great was their preoccupation with their conversation they did not notice a slight scuffle as they entered, nor did the lawyer perceive a strange bulge in the heavy tapestried curtains that hung by the window.

"I tell you, Father," said Talbot Brookestone in an unusually heated voice, "the plans cannot be changed. Need I go through the reasons again? To change now at the eleventh hour will inevitably lead to complications and they may well lead to disaster."

"My friend," came the reply, and Andrew stood amazed as he heard a voice he recognized, "disaster lies in delay now. There are too many who interest themselves in our affairs. Twelve hours ago it was different, but we have learnt much this night. We must heed its warnings."

"What warnings? The night was ours. We've scotched the old snake, and the young one knows nothing. As for the meddling Redcoat, well, he will meddle no more. 'Twill be folly to be panicked now."

"The plans must be changed," replied the other relentlessly in a calm voice. "We shall start at twilight."

"But the men are tired. And they are disgruntled enough with all the night work."

"Pay them double. You will not miss it, and the King's coffers are deep. He knows how to reward his own."

"But our friends—how will they know?"

"By messengers whom you will send." The voice had hardened. "You will do well to remember, Brookestone, that in this operation I am the commanding officer." He thumped his fist on the desk at which he sat. "The plans will be changed. I shall leave with the first convoy at twilight. Messengers must leave within the hour to give warning. Our friend at the Tiger, is it not, will doubtless manage that. One more point. Should the plans fail, which I am confident they will not, the names of our friends must never be known. Are there any documents here which contain their names?"

"None. Those the officers had, we destroyed. Nicholas Mole's information died with him. The information is all in my head. The only written copy is safe in the Ludgate office, and I shall see that is destroyed tomorrow."

"Good. To dine now, mon ami." The warmth was returning to his voice. "I think I can stomach just one more toast to Brandy Nan."

Andrew heard them rise and leave the room. He peered out thankfully, and scratched vigorously at his leg. Why do itches always come at the most awkward times? His mind awhirl with conjectures about the conversation he had just heard, he darted across to the door, eased it open and listened to their retreating footsteps. Quickly he left the room and soon found the staircase he sought. It was after the fourth door from the end of the corridor. Either his memory or Sophia's maths was at fault; Andrew suspected the latter.

His spirits were high as he creaked up the old wooden stairs, very different from the beautifully polished oak main stairs. So confident was he that he worried not a whit over the noise he was making. A long dark corridor stretched away to his right. The only light was provided by a small barred window opposite the top of the stairs at which he took his bearings. There was Lindfield Church spire overtopping the trees at the end of the village. Andrew thought quickly. He had had no help from Sophia about this part of the house. She imagined that his purposes ended with the discovery of the lawyer's room. Andrew had a good sense of direction. He turned to the right, went twenty yards down the corridor, and paused outside a door on his left. This should be the one. He listened. All was silence.

Cautiously he pulled the leather thong that raised the latch. It gave a slight click. Good, the door was not bolted. He pushed it open and then stopped in horror. For there, slumped in a chair, his mouth wide open, his eyes fast closed, was Andrew's opponent of the night before—Joe. The unexpectedness of seeing the wicked features again in such circumstances almost drew a cry of surprise from Andrew. He controlled himself. To his dismay Joe stirred, and Andrew's hand went to his sword, but it was a false alarm. Joe's slumbers were deep.

Andrew retreated and closed the door silently behind him. The experience had sobered him. He remembered against whom he was fighting; men who were ruthless, men who would commit murder without a second thought to gain their end, and their end was the overthrow of a kingdom and the overthrow of the Protestant faith that Andrew held dear. He breathed a prayer of thankfulness at his escape.

He knew he must be near the room he wanted, and he suspected that Joe's duties might well be those of a guard. In that case surely it must be the next room. He crept up to the door, found the leather thong, gave it a gentle tug and heard the latch click. He gave a push. The door did not budge. Andrew quietly lowered the latch. In the bad light he could not see what held the door, but he ran his fingers down it and at the bottom to his surprise and joy he found a great metal bolt. It was bolted on the outside. Andrew's heart thumped faster as he pulled the bolt back. What room needed a bolt on the outside— except a prison? He pulled at the latch and this time the door gave way.

As it swung open it revealed a bare room with one figure in it—the figure of Lieutenant Woodruff. Half-wakened from sleep by the entry of Andrew he was hardly recognizable as the smart young officer of the night before. He was half lying against the wall under the only window of the room. His cravat was little more than a rag, his shirt was ripped, and his trousers mud-stained and torn. He looked round as Andrew entered and his dazed eyes spoke his welcome. He sprang to his feet.

"Well done, Andrew," he said quietly. "I've been praying you would come, but there seemed little hope. Where is this?"

"Steadwell Hall."

"I thought so. That's why I left the sign." He picked

up a strip of red cloth which he had hung out of the window, the strip with which Joe had gagged him to keep quiet. "Full marks for seeing that."

"What . . . "began Andrew, who had many questions to ask.

"Explanations afterwards. We must get out of here first. How . . . What was that?" He interrupted himself at the sound of a bump followed by footsteps.

"It must be Joe," replied Andrew listening carefully. "He's in the next-door room and I think he's there to guard you. He was asleep a few moments ago."

"Well, he's not asleep now! Quick, we must make a dash for it."

Andrew, who knew their position better than the Lieutenant, realized this would be useless. Joe was moving about and presumably would soon come to check on his prisoner. To escape they would have to pass Joe's room, and even if they succeeded he would quickly raise the alarm and Andrew had enough respect for his opponents' powers to know they would be fortunate indeed if they lived for long enough to tell their tale. An idea flashed into his head.

"Follow me!" he commanded, and the urgency in his voice compelled obedience. He led Woodruff out into the passage and closed the door behind them. They blinked in the darkness and Andrew was just stooping to rebolt the door when the latch of the next door clicked. Joe was coming out.

"Back against the wall," breathed Andrew, and they flattened themselves against the wall just beyond the door. Andrew was banking on one hope; that Joe's eyes would be slow in accustoming themselves to the poor light, but his hand was on his sword—just in case. Joe's door opened and cast a beam of light across the passage, but that was ten yards from them and Joe's heavy form lumbered out. He began to stumble up the corridor.

He reached the door; three yards away stood Andrew. Joe fumbled at the bolt, uttered an exclamation of surprise and pushed the door open on an empty room. Andrew sprang forward out of the darkness and hurled himself against Joe's bulk. With a shout of surprise, Joe, caught off balance, pitched forward into the room and thumped heavily to the ground. Andrew grabbed the door, pulled it shut and bolted it.

"Come on," he said. The Lieutenant needed no second bidding. They sped down the corridor. An angry roar from behind told them that Joe had recovered from his misfortune, but Andrew noted with pleasure that the roars faded quickly as they hurried down the stairs. If the rest of the household were at dinner it would be some time before Joe's shouts would be heard.

They reached the top of the stairs just in time to see Talbot Brookestone stride across the hall to the door of the room set apart for Sophia's lessons. He tapped on the door and entered. Before the door shut Andrew heard the opening of their conversation.

"Alone, Sophia? And where is your gallant young tutor?" he asked.

"I know not, sir," came Sophia's clear reply. She made no attempt to keep her dislike of the lawyer out of her voice.

And then the door closed. Andrew was sorely tempted to return to Sophia's aid, but he knew this would be putting himself within the clutches of the lawyer, a risk that could not be taken now. He signalled to Lieutenant Woodruff, who was crouching behind the oak panelling at the top of the stairs, and they hurried down the stairs across the hall to the front door. In a few seconds they were outside—free. In his elation Andrew did not forget to use a covered line of retreat from the Hall. They made for Peter's farm as fast as Woodruff could manage, for he was weak from exhaustion and lack of food. Twice he stumbled and fell on the rough path along which Andrew led him, but there was a streak of toughness and endurance in him, which none who had known him as the somewhat foppish officer in fashionable society could have suspected. He kept up gamely and arrived at the farm to find a well-satisfied Peter about to drive in his herd to be milked— well satisfied because of the excellent price he had obtained for the hay that had been carted away that day.

"Some food, Peter, for the Lieutenant. He hasn't found the food at the Hall satisfactory." Peter was slowly framing his questions when Andrew continued, "Food first, talk afterwards, Peter!"

Peter, slightly surprised at the authoritative ring in Andrew's voice, nevertheless obeyed, and busied himself with an occupation which he loved second only to farming.

"You can see why Peter doesn't marry," said Andrew cheerfully to the Lieutenant, who was sitting still and white on a wooden stool, the most comfortable piece of furniture Peter's house could offer. "He couldn't bear to have anyone else do the cooking."

The great open fire at the end of the kitchen blazed round Peter's cooking pots. Delicious smells began to reach Lieutenant Woodruff and Andrew, making their hunger almost unbearable. In half-an-hour they were hard at work on the Roast Beef, Chicken Pies, Butter-sauce, and Cabbage which Peter laid before them. This was followed by Quince Tart, which Lieutenant Woodruff swore was the finest he'd ever eaten.

Explanations were just beginning when voices were heard outside. Andrew peered through the window, and turned in horror.

"It's Joe and four others. They're armed with pistols."

The somnolence which had fallen on Lieutenant Woodruff since dining vanished. He leapt up.

"Where can we hide? This is not the time for a battle."

Peter pointed to the worn stone staircase which led to his bedroom. Lieutenant Woodruff and Andrew disappeared, Andrew clutching his knife and fork as he went. The voices grew louder and then came a great hammering on the door. Peter moved slowly to open it. Sam, his huge cow-dog, growled in the corner.

"Have you seen two men? They came this way. They're wanted by the Sheriff."

"Eh?" said Peter. Sam growled more loudly.

"Two men! Have you seen them?" bellowed Joe.

"Are you the Sheriff's men?" asked Peter.

"Aye, and we're going to search your house."

Peter moved back slightly.

"You are welcome, sirs. I always help those who keep law and order, but I should warn you...." And there he stopped.

"Warn us?" said Joe who had stepped into the kitchen. "Warn us of what?"

"Of my dog," said Peter. "I'm afraid he's dangerous, especially when he sees pistols. They frighten him."

Joe had been observing the approach of the growling Sam somewhat uneasily. "Get back, you brute," he said, turning his pistol playfully towards the dog. The effect was instantaneous. With a fearsome snarl Sam sprang forward, teeth gleaming. Joe almost fell backwards through the doorway in the rapidity of his retreat. Sam took up a position on the threshold.

"I'll shoot him," said Joe, but even as he raised his pistol he saw Sam's dislike of firearms about to show itself in action. He lowered the pistol.

"We're wasting our time here," said Jesse, eyeing Sam with disfavour. "Old Foot's house is just over yonder. That's where they would have made for."

Joe was not reluctant to agree to give up the intended search of the farmhouse.

"If I see that dog again I'll shoot him," was his parting

shot. Sam snarled back defiantly. As Peter closed the door a slow, broad smile spread over his face.

"Here y'are, Sam, old boy," he said tossing him a succulent meat bone. "You've earned it."

Lieutenant Woodruff and Andrew had heard enough of the proceedings to enjoy the joke. They gleefully rejoined Peter. Seated round the fire they brought him up to date with the situation.

"Those coffins leave Lindfield at dusk to-night, then," said Woodruff. "That gives us four hours to make our plans."

"But how will they move them?" asked Andrew.

That indeed was a problem he'd been pondering for some time.

"I have my ideas about that, and think perhaps it will not be impossible to see they do not leave Lindfield," replied the officer mysteriously. "Peter will help me."

"Aye, that I will if . . ." began Peter.

"And what about me?" interrupted Andrew rudely.

"Patience, Andrew. Your part will be a big one, in fact it will be the biggest of the lot. Peter and I will catch small fish, you will catch whales." In this way did Woodruff soothe the ruffled Andrew, and then sitting forward and staring at the glowing coals in the fire he expounded the position and his plans to deal with it.

"If we succeed in preventing the Jacobites getting the arms to their destination, well, that will mean one up to us and gloomy faces at St. Germain for a while, but not for long. England is a prize worth fighting for, and the Pretender is not without those who nightly drink a toast to King James III and who even now are expecting consignments of arms with which to win him his throne. It's useless to extract one tooth when the whole mouth is rotten."

"Speak plainly," interrupted Andrew, who had a suspicion the Lieutenant was fobbing him off with high sounding phrases. He need have had no such fears.

"I will, my friend. There is, thanks to the failure of Captain Canting and myself, only one copy now left of the document that names the traitors who are expecting these arms."

"That's true," said Andrew. "Lawyer Brookestone said that plainly enough this afternoon."

"Right. And where is that document?"

"I've told you. In Lawyer Brookestone's office in London."

"And that is where *you* are going, Andrew."

"What? To London, but surely . . . " began Andrew.

"Listen. There is no time for argument. As soon as the plotters run into trouble at Lindfield a messenger will be despatched at once to London to destroy those papers. But those papers will not be destroyed. By the time he arrives they will have gone. You will have them." Woodruff, his pale face ruddy now from the warmth of the fire, turned to look at Andrew.

"You can ride?"

"Yes, he can ride," Peter said. "He won two races on the common last May day."

"Well, you must win another today, and if all goes well you'll have a good three hours' start."

"But a horse? I've no horse, and none of Peter's would get me to London this week." Andrew was beginning to take to the idea. He grinned wickedly at Peter as he said this.

"I think I can manage the horse, Andrew," said Lieutenant Woodruff. "There's a fine beast at the Tiger that will hold its own against any horse in Sussex." He rose and thanked Peter warmly for his hospitality. "Early milking time this afternoon, Peter, and on duty by the Tiger half-an-hour before dusk."

"Aye, aye sir," said Peter cheerfully, giving a poor imitation of an army salute.

They said their farewells. "God bless you, Andrew," said Peter fervently as they parted. Lieutenant Woodruff and Andrew trudged across the heath towards the High Street and the Tiger. A cloak borrowed from Peter covered the deplorable state of Lieutenant Woodruff's clothing. After discussing plans a silence fell on them. A slight smile played round Andrew's lip. Lieutenant Woodruff noticed it.

"Come on, out with it. There's one thing you haven't told me yet. Who was the man whom you heard speaking with the lawyer this afternoon?"

Andrew smiled. "I was waiting for you to ask me that. I'll tell you on one condition."

"Well?"

"That I may be the one to settle accounts with him."

"I can't promise that, Andrew, but if it is possible I shall do my best to grant your wish." He looked curiously at Andrew. "But why do you aim your arrow at him? He may well be the chief plotter, but he has not done you any harm."

Andrew smiled grimly. "He's more than a plotter, Lieutenant. He's a murderer. He murdered Daniel."

11

AT this juncture it may be wondered how the officer in charge of operations, Captain Canting, had been spending the hours which had brought so many changes of fortune to his junior officer. It must be admitted that his night was not a restful one. His excuse would be that there was an exceptional amount of noisy traffic around the inn during the night—exceptional even for a popular coaching inn—and that whenever he succeeded in dozing off a violent rumble or hoarse shout would pull him back to wakefulness. Indeed he made this point most strongly in an interview with the innkeeper, which will be related shortly. But these disturbances must not be given all the blame, for the Captain's own excesses of the evening before were guilty parties, too. His intoxicated brain remained active even when his eyes closed in fitful sleep. Wild imaginings filled his dreams. He was at Ramillies. The French were charging. The men at his side suddenly disappeared. He was alone. The French muskets volleyed. He awoke perspiring profusely. To sleep again. He was in a coach, alone. Galloping hooves behind. Highwaymen. "Faster," he screamed to the coachman. But the highwaymen gained. Two masked faces, one at each window with pistols levelled at his head. They fired. The Captain awoke with a start. Loud noises came from the stable yard behind the inn. The Captain cursed them and rolled hopefully over again.

Thus it was that when the bright rays of the morning sun streamed into his room dazzling him as he opened his eyes, his temper was at its most savage. He strode to the window to see the cause of the nocturnal disturbances, but it was a peaceful scene which met his angry gaze. The horses in their stalls gazed placidly out on the new day, while the ostlers hurried about the yard bearing pails of water to their charges. Having dressed, he banged on the door of Woodruff's room. There was no reply. He walked in and was slightly taken aback to find that the Lieutenant had not slept in his bed that night. He tried to collect his thoughts, but a muzziness stifled his efforts. Breakfast. That was what he needed. He'd be all right after some breakfast. And then he would see the landlord. He had a lot to say to him about the disturbances of last night. And then the events of the day before came dimly into his mind. Mother Willis' words. "The Land-lord of the Tiger is no lover of Brandy Nan." Yes, he must see this landlord. He had quite a few questions to ask him.

And strangely enough at exactly the same time the landlord was planning an interview with him.

At breakfast he snapped viciously at the waiter and found fault with all that was laid before him. The waiter inquired whether Lieutenant Woodruff would be coming down to breakfast, but received no answer beyond a snarl. The Captain did not like to admit his ignorance of the whereabouts of his Junior Officer, and he felt most aggrieved that Lieutenant Woodruff had not fully informed him of his movements. Why should he, Captain Canting, have to bear the whole brunt of the investiga-tion? Woodruff was again the useless young pup, a fact which he had recognized from the start.

"Tell the landlord I wish to see him at once," he barked at the waiter who was clearing away the remnants of the meal.

His command was carried out. The landlord's eyes gleamed when he received the message.

"The landlord is working in the back-room, sir," reported the waiter, "and will be happy to see you now if it suits your convenience." A grunt from the Captain suggested that it did and the waiter led him across the stone-flagged hall to the back-room. The Captain entered.

It was not his idea of a suitable place for his reception. It was more like a small barn than a room. The furniture was scanty and of the rudest. In the middle was a roughly made table at which the landlord sat on a stool. On the table were papers and on the side walls two strong ropes that stretched from floor to ceiling. Canting did not notice these. The landlord rose.

"Forgive me for receiving you here," he said, but there was no note of apology in his voice. He rose and directed the Captain to a chair, the only other article of furniture in the room. Captain Canting sat down heavily and dimly noticed that the floor swayed beneath him at his impact on the chair.

He launched into a long complaint about the noises of the night. The landlord was placatory. A large consignment of beer had arrived unexpectedly late in the night. It was a most unusual occurrence and one which would not happen again. He himself would see to that.

During the conversation the Captain had an unhappy feeling he was not doing well. The eyes of the landlord never left him, and the muzziness in his head blurred all clear thought.

"Is that all, sir?" asked the landlord and there was a sneer in his voice.

The Captain hesitated and then there came over him the feeling he hated more than any other—the feeling that he was being mocked. Very well. He would show this landlord he would not be mocked with impunity.

"Yes. There is more. I want you to answer a few questions."

The landlord said nothing.

"First, have you any large quantities of arms and ammunition stored here?" This was a complete shot in the dark. The truth was that it was the first question that came into his mind. He had no reason to suppose the existence of arms at the Tiger. But shot in the dark or not, it appeared to score a hit. The landlord, white-faced and eyes blazing, sprang to his feet.

"Let her go," he yelled.

Almost before he could move Captain Canting felt the floor shudder and move beneath him. He tried to spring forward, but his foot found no hold. He was falling, falling, and as he fell his head crashed on the edge of the floor. He thudded down below, unconscious.

"Pull her back," shouted the landlord. The gaping hole in front of him was filled again by the floorboards, swung upward by a pulley. Patrick, a broad brawny servant, entered in his shirt-sleeves. "Ah, he went down as beautiful as the barrels of beer does. It's a wonderful invention of yours, it is to be sure. But it's thirsty work, it is, with that pulley. I'm that dry I could drink a barrel myself, to be sure."

"Draw yourself a pint and not a drop more," snapped the landlord.

"Ah, you're a generous man. 'Tis just what I need now. A generous man, to be sure." And with that he went in search of his pint. The landlord stood thoughtfully by his table. A new expression spread across his face. It was not a pleasant one to behold.

It was some minutes before the Captain, stunned by his fall, moved at all, and then he moved gingerly, groaning as he did so. Nevertheless the fury in his heart was such that he was soon on his feet exploring his prison. It was a dark stone underground cellar. At one end were piled a dozen or so barrels of beer, at the other was a large chute which the Captain guessed rightly was used to run the beer barrels into the cellar through the same entrance that he had involuntarily used. The walls offered him no hope of escape. He realized his only chance lay in the wooden roof. But that was ten feet above his head. He set to work to move the chute to a position from which he could start operations.

It was some six hours later when Lieutenant Woodruff and Andrew reached the Tiger. In a short time Woodruff felt and indeed looked a new man. Arrayed in his best uniform and wig he was once again recognizable as one of the frequenters of a London Coffee House. A glance in a small mirror afforded him much satisfaction. He was one who felt his best if he looked his best, and he certainly looked smart now, with his gleaming white neckband, red coat with its blue facings, his blue waistcoat, white trousers and shining boots. Andrew watched the transformation with interest, idly wondering whether a career in the Army would suit him. The uniform was magnificent.

"Well, Andrew. It's time you were on your way," said the officer, every inch an officer now. "You'll have three hours' start if we play our part successfully, and possibly more. You know what to do if you can't find the papers?"

Andrew nodded. "Lock the office as far as possible and hold it against all comers."

"Yes. If anyone is there when you arrive, lie low. They will probably leave shortly, if Sophia is accurate."

"She was most definite that no one slept in the building; Carson has to stay in lodgings nearby."

"Good." Lieutenant Woodruff walked across to his chest and unlocked it. From the bottom he drew out a handsome pistol, which he handed to Andrew. Andrew took it gingerly.

"It won't bite you," laughed Woodruff. "It's not even primed."

"But I've never used one of these," protested Andrew.

"Don't worry on that account. The Jacobites don't know that, and even if they did they would still treat you with a healthy respect. Give it to me. It's easy enough. Watch." He swung the pistol up to the full extent of his left arm, sighted it at a weird carving over the chimney, and gently squeezed the trigger. "Nothing to it, you see," he added encouragingly. He omitted to mention the fact that he himself rarely hit anything he aimed at, and that his life had been saved at the only duel in which he had ever taken part because his opponent was just as nervous as he. They had both missed by wide margins. Andrew took the pistol and practised taking aim. Then he was instructed in the art of priming it and shown the importance of a steady pressure on the trigger. He was an apt pupil and was soon enthusing over this addition to his armoury. Then a though struck him.

"But what about you? Have you another pistol?"

"No. I lost that one's brother in my skirmish with Joe, but don't worry yourself over that. I'm sure Captain Canting will oblige me with one of his should they prove neccessary."

"Where is this Captain of yours? I want to meet him." The tone of Andrew's voice did not suggest the meeting would be a particularly pleasant one.

"I don't know," said Woodruff thoughtfully. "I should like to know very much. It may be that the landlord can help me. But, Andrew, my friend, time is passing. You must be away."

Andrew sprang up from the chair and thrust the pistol which he had been fingering proudly into his belt.

"There is one thing I'd like you to do, Andrew, before you go," said the Lieutenant.

"Well?" replied Andrew.

"Pray. Pray for both of us. Just as you and Peter prayed beside Daniel Foot's bed."

A flash of surprise in Andrew's eyes when Woodruff began his request rapidly changed to one of joy.

"Yes, I'll pray," he said and he knelt down by the chair. Lieutenant Woodruff knelt beside him. Andrew prayed simply. He asked God to be with them and give them courage for what lay ahead.

They rose.

"Thank you, Andrew," said the officer. "Wait here and I'll see about your horse." He disappeared briskly and Andrew wandered idly to the window. He soon saw Woodruff stride into the courtyard below. An ostler ran to speak with him. A few words from the officer were enough. The ostler went to the stables and soon led out a large piebald horse, Woodruff's mount of the day before. The Lieutenant glanced up at the window and seeing Andrew motioned him to come down.

In a short time Andrew was in the saddle. Woodruff squeezed his hand as they parted. A smile, a wave and Andrew was away, galloping northwards for London.

Woodruff stood watching him as he disappeared beyond the church and then turned back towards the Tiger. The landlord who had been observing the proceedings with a considerably puzzled expression stepped forward to meet him.

"Good afternoon, Lieutenant," he said, a broad smile revealing his misshapen and blackened teeth. "Will you honour me by taking a drink with me? Some excellent beer arrived last night, and what could be better than that you should join me in being the first to taste it."

Lieutenant Woodruff's brain was working fast as he graciously accepted the invitation. They entered the bar and there set out on the table were two great tankards of beer.

"You won't have tasted anything as good as this for a long time, Lieutenant," said the landlord as he handed Woodruff on of the tankards. "I'm sorry Captain Canting isn't here to sample it," observed the officer. "He is more of a connoisseur. Have you seen him recently?" The question came sharply.

There was a slight pause, duly noted by Woodruff, before the landlord answered.

"He went out early and I haven't seen him since."

"In which direction?"

"That I couldn't say, sir," replied the landlord, his tone becoming distinctly less friendly. "Come, sir, let us drink a toast to ..."

"By all means, but I'd like one matter settled first. Would you ask the ostlers if Captain Canting has taken a horse today?"

"The Captain went on foot."

"Nevertheless I shall drink the happier if I have certain information about it. I should be much obliged if you made enquiries." There was an unmistakable ring of authority in Woodruff's voice.

The landlord slowly put down his tankard.

"Very well, sir," he said, his voice back to its usual surliness. "I'll see the ostlers." There was a note of menace in the last statement.

He left the bar, and Lieutenant Woodruff watching carefully through the window saw him walk across the stable yard and call the ostlers together. He ran to the door. There was no one about. He returned to the two tankards and made a quick change in their positions. The landlord, he saw, was returning across the yard followed by the three ostlers, and each ostler he noted was carrying a stout cudgel. Woodruff took the precaution of unbolting the door which led out to the main street. It appeared that a change of tactics might be necessary.

However the landlord entered alone, though shufflings in the corridor outside suggested that Woodruff was not the only one to take precautions. There was a smile on the landlord's lips.

"The Captain has taken no horse today, sir. My ostlers are quite certain about that. In fact, sir, you're the only one that has taken a horse today."

"Thank you, landlord, for your trouble."

"No trouble, sir," the landlord replied and seizing his tankard he proposed a loyal toast. Woodruff did the same. They both drank. Suddenly the landlord tore the tankard from his lips and crashed it on to the table, beer swilling wildly over the sides. His face turned white.

"You ..." he snarled, turning to the Lieutenant, but the sentence was never to be completed. His knees crumpled under him and he fell forward to the ground.

Woodruff called the ostlers. They entered suspiciously, but their suspicions changed to bewilderment.

"His drink did not agree with him," snapped the Lieutenant. "Get him to his room."

The ostlers looked from the motionless body of the landlord to the erect officer who was standing with his hand on the hilt of his sword. They did not hesitate. Having sheepishly laid down their cudgels, they shuffled across to the landlord and carried him out.

"Send for a doctor at once," was Woodruff's final command. As he watched them go, however, it was not the landlord he was thinking about, but Andrew.

"God be with you, Andrew," he murmured.

12

ANDREW soon found as Lieutenant Woodruff had done
that the horse under him was an exceptional one. In two
and a half hours the North Downs were behind him. He
had met several coaches thundering southwards and
groups of riders who eyed him with surprise. It was unusual to ride alone. The road he travelled varied in quality, most tracts of it being a mere path of mud or fen,
others paved with small cobbles. The art of roadmaking
was still a lost one in England. But his horse never slackened its steady pace. All surfaces seemed to come alike to
Cromwell. His mud-bespattered flanks gleamed with
sweat, but still he galloped through the peaceful villages,
past clusters of cottages, some little more than huts, and
farm buildings often with their newly-built manor houses,
simple but dignified, surrounded by well-kept parks.
Through woods, commons, and heathland on which
grazed "starved tod-bellied runts neither fit for the dairy
nor the yoke," cattle which Peter Virley would never have
countenanced, went Andrew on Cromwell.

His spirits were high. This was better than Latin verse,
he thought, as he looked over the fertile Surrey plains
towards the greatest city in the world. He was inspired by
the story of his father which he had at last learnt from
Daniel. He knew that he was fighting for the same cause as
his father, and he knew it was worth fighting for. He also

knew that his mission was dangerous and that his enemies would stop at nothing to make sure the incriminating documents never reached official hands; but though he loved his life he did not fear death. He had seen Daniel die with such quiet confidence that death held no terrors for him now.

And then when London Bridge was but five miles away the sinking sun was overclouded by heavy clouds rolling in from the south-west. A chill filled the air. Glancing over his shoulder Andrew saw a shadowy veil hanging over the downs. Rain. Before long the first spots were falling round him. The sky was dark. Andrew shivered and pulled his cloak more tightly round him as the rain began to beat down. It was the uncertainty rather than the glory of the April day that was now evident. The track along which Cromwell galloped quickly became a muddy river treacherous to feet and hooves. At the top of a sharp incline Cromwell stumbled for the first time and half fell. Andrew was able to leap clear. Cromwell scrambled to his feet. As Andrew soothed him and led him gently forward he saw to his dismay that he limped. Cromwell could carry him no further.

However, he had played his part nobly. Andrew was now less than five miles from London. The road was liberally supplied with coaching houses and inns of varying quality, and Andrew led Cromwell on till he came to one. The innkeeper agreed to take the horse in and keep him till Andrew returned. He was unable to supply him with another horse. Andrew paid two shillings with promise of twice as much when he returned, and did not leave till he had seen Cromwell comfortably settled in a stable. Then Andrew set out on the last stage of the journey. He decided against searching for a fresh mount. The distance was not great, and if all had gone well in Lindfield he had a good start.

An hour later, drenched but still cheerful, Andrew set foot on London Bridge, the only bridge across the Thames in those days. It was a remarkable one, for each side of the narrow roadway across the river was lined with shops and houses, and indeed the bridge was as busy a shopping centre as any in London. As he passed under the great arched gateway on to the bridge, Andrew's heart beat faster. The dark, smelly street contrasted unfavourably with the open heaths across which he had come. The teeming rain meant that the bridge was almost deserted, and inside the lofty houses lantern lights were twinkling. Andrew's discomfort was eased by the realization that the rain was slackening. In his mind he was running over Sophia's instructions. He had still a mile to go in what to him was unknown country. Though it was only twilight the streets were all dark, and near the river at least the buildings were often tumbledown with untiled roofs and walls which bulged alarmingly.

The rain stopped. Andrew squelched on towards his destination near Ludgate. A sound of voices and laughter came to his ears. He stopped and looked along the street. Dim figures were moving rapidly to and fro across West Cheap. The shouts were of merriment but intermingled with them Andrew caught the sound of hoarse cries for help. He hurried forward.

"The Mohocks!" he thought. "Mohocks" was the name given to lawless bands of young men, many of them of the best families, who terrorized the citizens of London with their nocturnal activities. They waylaid, tormented, and often wounded respectable citizens, they overturned coaches, they burned sedan-chairs and ransacked shops and had murdered two watchmen—and all this not for gain but for adventure. Angry deputations to Parliament had produced little; the Mohocks still roamed the streets and the meagre forces of law and order were helpless against them. And soon it was not only at night that they worked. Emboldened by success the Mohocks won further notoriety by daring exploits by day. The mere whisper of the word "Mohock" was used by parents to frighten naughty children, and the parents themselves were careful never to venture out if it was rumoured that the Mohocks were abroad.

Andrew was right. It was the Mohocks, and as he neared the scene he saw more clearly their devilish work. In the middle of the road the small figure of an old man was dancing, while circling him some four masked Mohocks made play with their swords, forcing him to leap from one side to another to avoid their playful but dangerous thrusts. The Mohocks laughed heartily at the old man's antics, his cries for help seemed unavailing. The street was deserted, and in the houses, though here and there a dim light shone through the windows, there were no signs of life. Other Mohocks were busy in a shop above which hung the sign "Bernard Syncleere, Tailour." From the shop they carried out coats and hats and wigs, doubtless for use later in the evening.

"'Tis not often we cut the cloth of a tailor," screamed one of the Mohocks, lunging at the old man.

"'Tis poor material," cried another. "See how it rips."

Andrew hesitated no longer. With drawn sword he flung himself on the tormentors, who had been so occupied with the unfortunate tailor that they did not notice his approach. At first they fell back at the unexpected and not unskilled onslaught. But soon it was Andrew who was on the defensive. The odds were hopeless, and his opponents were as good swordsmen as he. To give the Mohocks their due, they did not try to kill as they probably could have done but they drove him back against the building, mocking him as he retreated.

"He has no wig," cried one. "Let us fit him out."

"Then he must be a Tory," cried another.

"Death to all Tories," shouted a third, lunging towards Andrew.

"Come, try on this wig. 'Tis made for swollen heads," said the first, advancing towards Andrew with a handsome white periwig. Andrew struck it from his hand with a neat flick of his sword. The Mohock swore wildly. The attack was renewed with more serious intent and it would have gone ill with Andrew had not Bernard Syncleere, the unfortunate tailor, shown himself to be a man of spirit. Andrew's intervention had allowed him to escape from his tormentors, but instead of slipping away to safety he ran down the street lustily calling his neighbours by name to repel the Mohocks. Goaded by his shouts, and perhaps encouraged by the sound of clashing steel which showed that the Mohocks were not having it all their own way, his neighbours began to appear at windows, and doors were unbolted and thrown open.

On one side of Syncleere's shop was the shop of Maximus Pringle, the greengrocer. Syncleere himself made an inspired suggestion, and in a matter of seconds a vigorous volley of vegetables crashed among the Mohocks.

Andrew's main opponent was felled by a huge turnip propelled by the brawny arms of Maximus Pringle. Carrots, cabbages, swedes, and potatoes flew thickly and indiscriminately. Andrew himself was hit several times, but succeeded in disengaging himself. His assailants made a half-hearted and futile attempt to rush the green-grocer's shop, but then becoming alarmed at the hornet's nest they had roused, for they were now being pelted and showered from every window within range, they retreated up the street towards St. Paul's. Jeers pursued them.

Syncleere ruefully surveyed his clothes which lay in the muddy vegetable strewn street. His wife comforted him with the reflection that events might have turned out worse had not this brave young gentleman, and she pointed at the blushing Andrew, come upon the scene.

Andrew refused all their offers of hospitality, but made one request. He asked for a lantern, which he promised to return at the first opportunity. His request was gladly granted, and after a warm farewell Andrew resumed his journey up West Cheap to St. Paul's. After the darkness of the London street the sudden magnificence of the Cathedral standing out black against the deep blue night sky took his breath away.

He knew his lead over the Jacobites must have been shortened by his encounter with the Mohocks, but he still had time in hand. He turned aside into St. Paul's, walked up the great steps and into the mighty cathedral, and there he knelt in a pew and prayed, thanking God for his deliverance from danger and committing the future to Him.

Then out into the dark streets of London into Ludgate. He hastened over the wet cobbles, glistening in the dull lights from the narrow windows. The first turning on the left. Andrew soon came to it—a narrow, forbidding alley. The second doorway on the left. He felt his way down and soon came to the second doorway. He drew his lantern from its hiding-place under his cloak and let its beams fall on the door. Carved on a small board nailed to the door was the simple inscription "James Brookestone and Son." Andrew sighed with relief. He had reached his destination. Back under his cloak went the lantern as he stepped back to survey the building. In the room above the door a light was burning. Andrew stared up in dismay. Surely no one could still be working. What if a watchman were left here all night? What hope would there be of forcing the door if a guard were on the alert inside?

He tried in vain to see the occupant of the room. All

he could see were the beams criss-crossing a dusty ceiling. Then a thought occurred to him. If it were a late worker or even a guard it was just possible the street door might not yet be bolted, and in that case now was the time to make his entry. In this way the dangers attending the forcing of a locked door on the street would be avoided. He slipped across to the doorway and gently tried the handle. With a slight click Andrew heard the latch disengage. The door was open. It creaked as Andrew opened it wide enough to slip in and it creaked again as he shut it. Surely the person upstairs must have heard it. For seconds that seemed like hours to Andrew, he waited, not daring to move, but no sound came from above.

Plucking up courage he allowed some rays from the lantern to escape from the enfolding cloak. He was in a small hall. Straight ahead was a staircase leading up to the room above the door, the room where the documents were kept. To the right of the staircase was a narrow passage leading to a room at the back and off which were two rooms to the right. He was just calculating his next move when there was a sound of footsteps above.

A momentary panic seized Andrew. He had been heard. The whole scheme could be ruined if his presence were discovered now. He dared not use his lantern again as he groped his way forward in the gloomy hall. Under the stairs he felt a small alcove. As he slipped into its shelter the door above opened. Covering the lantern with his cloak, Andrew drew his sword. Slowly and heavily the footsteps descended the stairs, which creaked over Andrew's head. A light gradually filled the hall. He had a lantern. This took away Andrew's last hope. If the owner of the lantern turned when he reached the foot of the stairs he could not fail to see Andrew. Now for it. Andrew tightened his grip on his sword. The footsteps reached the bottom, and did not turn. Their owner was going out. Andrew, almost overcome with relief, incautiously peered out as he heard the door being opened. He saw in the doorway the dark silhouette of someone he knew well, Carson Pride.

The door shut. Andrew noted that Carson had not locked it. Carson's footsteps echoed down the alley. Then all was silence. Andrew emerged from his alcove excited and yet uneasy. His mind pondered the problem of Carson, a problem that had often recurred, since Carson's strange visit to Daniel. How far was Carson involved in the plot? Carson's unfriendly and unnatural behaviour, and his association with Brookstone, all suggested he was implicated and yet ... but Andrew reined in his wandering thoughts. He must act quickly. The door had not been locked. That might well mean that Carson would return or possibly that someone else was expected.

He climbed the stairs and pushed open the door of the office. The sight that met his eyes surprised him. There were the usual features of a lawyer's office: the shelves lined with musty brown-backed tomes, dealings of man with man dehydrated into print; there were rows of quill pens and polished inkstands, there were the heavy ledgers filled daily with fresh figures by industrious clerks, but what surprised Andrew was the untidy state of the room. It was almost as if the room had already been searched. The table and floor were covered with a litter of documents, and an old iron-bound chest with a mighty lock stood gaping open with its contents disarrayed, and at the far end of the room, most surprising of all, an ill-done portrait of James II had swung an inch or two out from the wall as if it were the door of a cupboard.

Andrew hastened across to it and found that indeed it

was. Its hinges worked noiselessly as Andrew pulled His Majesty further from the wall, revealing a deep-set shelved cupboard, filled with yet more documents.

After making sure there were no further hiding-places Andrew decided to start in this cupboard. After all, what more suitable guard for Jacobite documents could there be than His late Majesty, King James II? He pulled out the first pile and began to peruse their contents, and as he worked the question that kept running through his mind was "What was Carson doing here?"

13

LINDFIELD High Street was unusually crowded late on that April afternoon. From the pond to the Tiger there were groups of women talking together while children scampered round them. The noisiest group was one in which Old Mother Willis was playing the role of leader, and this group was situated directly outside the Tiger. George Bailey the Carpenter had left his work in his dark workshops and with his two apprentices stood enjoying the April sunshine. The two apprentices hardly knew what to make of this unexpected break. Bailey, a wonderful craftsman himself, demanded the highest standard from his apprentices, and woe betide the luckless boy he found idling! A release from the bench in working hours was a new experience.

The ostlers from the Red Lion, who claimed to groom the best coach-horses in Sussex, formed another lively party, and they too took up their stand not far from the Tiger.

Those who knew the irritability of the Landlord of the Tiger waited hopefully for his angry eruption from his inn to drive away the loiterers, but the landlord never came.

Old men stood in quieter parties muttering among themselves; some young lads from the farms formed an uproarious gang shouting insults at all who passed by.

A stranger to the village might have been excused for

imagining this to be market-day or even the day of the famous Lindfield fair, but he would have been wrong. It was neither. Why then such a crowd of idlers in the hours that were given for work? Why then were the plough and the loom and the saw laid aside? It is unlikely that one of the people mentioned could have given a satisfactory answer. They hardly knew themselves. Yet that afternoon a rumour had spread through Lindfield with the swiftness and deadliness of a forest fire. The rumour was vague, and took many different forms as it engulfed the village, but inside one hour there was scarcely a soul in the village who did not know that something strange and exciting was due to happen in Lindfield, and there was scarcely one soul who was not determined to see it happen. Excitement was a rare ingredient in village life. Over every group, young and old, hung an air of expectancy.

When the rumour had been more definite the name of the Tiger had been mentioned more than once, and so it was that gradually the main body of villagers drifted up towards that inn.

From a window in the inn Lieutenant Woodruff surveyed the scene with a satisfaction that came from seeing a job well done. Looking down the road he saw the crowds drawing back in respect for two figures who were making their way up towards the Tiger. The Lieutenant tensed with interest. From Andrew's description he could guess who they were. One was Talbot Brookestone, the other his mysterious friend, Dr. Carter. The lawyer was known and feared in Lindfield and he received many respectful bows and curtseys. Even the farm lads held their wagging tongues as the two gentlemen strode past. Lieutenant Woodruff noticed without surprise that they were both armed with swords and pistols.

They made straight for the Tiger, and the officer could hear their voices below, at first calm and then seemingly angry or agitated. He could guess the reason why. He had seen nothing more of the landlord since he was carried out, and had been too busy himself to make enquiries beyond a brief question to the sullen but frightened chief ostler who had answered that he was very ill. The disappearance of the Captain worried him. No one in the village seemed to have seen him that day, but Lieutenant Woodruff, whose opinion of his superior officer had steadily been growing less, had decided that any search for the Captain must be delayed till after the completion of the present operations.

And then a new sound was heard at the bottom of the High Street, the lowing of cattle as slowly up the street wandered a herd of bullocks driven forward by a dog. Behind them all walked Peter Virley and Sam.

There was nothing unusual about this. Round Lindfield there was much common ground where cattle could be grazed, and some of the best of this pasture lay to the north of the village. The bullocks were fine ones for those days, and doubtless helped to give "the roast beef of Old England" its world-wide reputation. They made their way unhurriedly, browsing on the grass at the roadside. Lieutenant Woodruff smiled as he saw them coming. It would not be long now.

Behind the inn sounds of activity could be heard; the turning of wagon wheels, the neighing of horses and the shouts of men. Lieutenant Woodruff picked up his three-cornered hat and carefully fitted it over his wig. Then he slipped out of his room.

The first of Peter's bullocks were jostling through the crowd outside the Tiger when a sudden rumbling attracted everyone's attention. Two horses dragging a huge wagon-load of hay moved slowly out of the alley by the Tiger into the street, followed by another with several more behind.

This was a common enough occurrence. Hay was in

great demand at the coaching inns and the stables of the wealthy up and down the country, and many Sussex farmers were able to sell their hay at a good profit to agents, especially if they kept it till late winter or spring. However, what was more unusual was that a herd of bullocks should be on the spot when this hay was temptingly dragged in front of them. And what was also unusual was that there seemed to be the large total of three carters to each wagon and each of the carters was armed with knife and pistol.

Now the leading bullocks had not been impressed by the quality or quantity of the grass they had found in Lindfield High Street, and now suddenly the delicious whiff of hay assailed their nostrils. Gratefully, their noses snuffing eagerly, they wheeled towards the wagons. The carters saw the danger. Angrily they raced round to drive the bullocks off. With munching mouths the bullocks retreated temporarily and then with a playful burst trotted behind the wagon and helped themselves to some more hearty mouthfuls. The onlookers prepared to enjoy themselves.

By this time the four wagons that had trundled out into the street had come to a standstill as the carters concentrated on repelling the bullocks. A fifth one was unable to leave the alley-way owing to the congestion in the street. The remainder of the bullocks hastened joyfully up. Angry carters chased the bullocks round the wagons, while the animals seemed to enter wholeheartedly into the spirit of the game. The ostlers from the Tiger armed with sticks joined the fray, but as soon as they had driven the beasts from one wagon they were feasting round the next, and so great was the attraction of the hay, that even blows affected them but little.

"Whose cows are these?" yelled a burly carter angrily to the delighted spectators.

They all motioned towards the figure of Peter who had just arrived outside the Tiger.

"Are these your cows?" the carter shouted.

Peter surveyed the confused scene placidly.

"Cows?" he queried.

"Yes, these cows," roared the carter.

"But they're not cows, they're bullocks."

The spectators roared with delight.

"Get them off, get them off," shouted the enraged carter.

"Oh, aye," replied Peter slowly. "Come on, Sam," he called to his dog. Sam ran up to his master most puzzled. He was receiving no commands he understood. He trotted behind Peter who ran amidst the bullocks waving his arms wildly. His action had little effect on the animals and if anything seemed to add to the confusion rather than lessen it.

Suddenly a figure appeared in the doorway of the Tiger. It was Talbot Brookestone. His eyes flashed from a face white with anger. In his hand he held a pistol. His hard voice rang out.

"Unless those beasts are called off they will be shot. I will count five. One."

"Ready with your pistols, men!" called out the chief carter, battling in vain with three hefty bullocks, who had made great inroads into the hay of the first wagon.

"Two!"

Peter was protesting loudly. The spectators were now quieter and stepping back from the scene. Events were taking an uglier turn.

"Three!"

Brookestone levelled the pistol at the bullock nearest him. The other carters did likewise. The chief carter, mad with rage, succeeded in driving the bullocks away from the first cart only to be smothered by an avalanche of hay. A laugh which rose from the crowd was suddenly checked by the harsh voice of the lawyer.

"Four!"

A new figure sprang into the chaos round the carts. Lieutenant Woodruff dashed from the Tiger, past Brookestone on the step and across to the first cart with its load half slipped to the ground. He sprang on to the cart, gaining a precarious foothold in the hay.

"Don't shoot," he cried, and such was the ring of authority in his voice that the levelled pistols were lowered —all except one, Talbot Brookestone's, which merely changed its target.

"People of Lindfield," he cried, "these carts must not be allowed to leave, they. . . ."

"The man's mad," shouted Talbot Brookestone. "Webb and Moore, bring him down."

Two of the carters moved towards the Lieutenant. In a flash he whipped out his sword which glinted in the dying rays of the sun. Webb and Moore hesitated. Lieutenant Woodruff continued addressing the crowd who were thronging the carts.

"These carts are carrying not hay, but. . . ."

"Bang!" A pistol shot was fired. Brookestone's pistol was smoking. The crowd growled angrily. The lawyer had made a mistake. In attempting to rid himself of one enemy he had made a hundred more.

"He's been hit," shouted someone, as Lieutenant Woodruff, wincing, clutched at his shoulder.

"A scratch!" he cried. "Watch this!" And he thrust his sword into the hay. It did not go far. A clank proclaimed the existence of a solid object. "These are arms and ammunition for the Jacobites. . . ."

"Shoot him!" screamed the lawyer, who had retreated into the Tiger before the menacing crowd, but only one of his men obeyed. Joe, the chief carter, levelled his pistol at his old enemy. There was murder in his eyes, but there was no murder. Before he pulled the trigger he was seized powerfully from behind. The pistol was wrenched from his grip. The crowd gasped with amazement for Joe's assailant was none other than the Vicar of Lindfield, the Reverend Thomas Bysshe. With his wig askew, and brandishing Joe's pistol in his hand, he sprang up beside Woodruff.

"You're wounded, my boy," he said, and indeed there was a tell-tale patch of red staining Woodruff's jacket by his left shoulder. "Get down."

But Woodruff heard nothing. All he knew was that he must get the crowd on his side. Then all Brookestone's men could do nothing.

"Pull these boxes out," he shouted, and several of the crowd sprang forward and tugged at the boxes where the landslide of hay had left them bare. The carters were disappearing into the crowd. Talbot Brookestone slammed the door of the Tiger in the face of the advancing crowd. There was a sudden tattoo of hoof beats as a horse burst from the alley beside the Tiger. The crowd scattered desperately as the horse shot among them. The rider crouched low over the horse's mane, but Woodruff knew who he was.

"Stop him," he cried, but it was too late. The rider was through the crowd, past the church and galloping northwards towards London.

In these desperate moments Sam, after a brief command from Peter, had rounded up the bullocks almost unnoticed and was driving them easily down the High Street towards Peter's farm. Peter himself was up on the cart beside Woodruff.

They all watched as three of the farm lads strained to open one of the coffins with an iron bar from the blacksmith's. With a splintering crash the lid was torn off.

Any doubts the crowd may still have had about Woodruff were dispersed. Held up before their eyes were the contents. Gleaming pistols and muskets with powder and shot.

"Listen," began the Lieutenant, but the scene began to dance before his eyes, a dizziness overcame him and he felt himself falling, falling. . . .

Peter clutched desperately but could not hold him, but the ground on to which the Lieutenant fell could not have been better prepared. A thick bed of hay received him softly. He was carried into the Tiger where willing hands dressed his wound.

Outside, the Reverend Thomas Bysshe, finding himself alone on the cart, had a moment of inspiration. He had prayed for many years for a larger congregation than the faithful dozen who congregated Sunday by Sunday. Was not this the answer? Never in his life before had he had a congregation like this and never probably would he have again. The pulpit was unorthodox and so was the occasion, but it was now or never.

"Listen, good people of Lindfield," he boomed out— and the people were listening. "These guns were destined to bring war to our land, to overthrow our Queen, God bless her, and her government, and to bring us under the yoke of the Stuarts again. But thanks to our brave young officer, God bless him, these things shall not be." He was encouraged by a cheer from the crowd.

The Vicar warmed to this theme. He reminded his listeners of the reign of the last of the Stuarts to rule, James II, when religious freedom had almost disappeared and the shadow of Rome had fallen across England again. He reminded them that the self-styled James III at St. Germain was an avowed Roman Catholic, and though he praised the Jacobite for his honest refusal to pretend otherwise in this matter, he warned his listeners that this very sincerity might well make Protestant martyrs, should he ever become James III in reality. The crowd murmured in approval. The Vicar continued, "If this plot had succeeded, the Church of England whose freedom has been won by the blood of your forefathers would once again be under yoke and your money would fill the coffers of Rome. That must not and shall not be."

And the people of Lindfield, most of whom hardly ever entered a church, cheered lustily, especially moved by the reference to their money. But the Vicar had not finished. "You will not lose your money to Rome, but there is something more precious that many of you have almost lost already—your souls! The riches of this earth with which you busy yourselves so much, the pleasures of this earth in which you seek to forget the woes, they are as light and worthless as a wisp of hay," and he plucked one from the cart beside him. The wisp floated down to the ground and all eyes watched it fall.

"All flesh is as grass and all the glory of men as the flower of grass," quoted the Vicar. "The grass withereth and the flower thereof falleth away, but the word of the Lord endureth for ever. Men, women and children of Lindfield, hear this word of the Lord before it is too late. Repent and believe!"

The crowd stirred uneasily. This was not so much to their liking, but there was power in the Vicar's voice and they stayed. "Turn from your sins which lead you on the pathway to hell. Believe the gospel of Jesus Christ. For God so loved the world that He gave His only begotten Son, that whosoever believeth in Him should not perish, but have everlasting life."

"The man's carried away!" came a voice from the crowd, but the events which followed soon showed that this was not the case. A sudden commotion in the yard behind the Tiger was followed by a hoarse shout, "They're escaping, Brookestone's escaping!"

Some men rushed down the alley-way, but were halted

by a pistol shot which splintered the fence by them. They paused irresolutely. The Vicar leapt from the cart and joined them.

In the yard Talbot Brookestone and four of the carters were mounted. The lawyer, a pistol smoking in his hand, had the desperate but dangerous look of a cornered rat. There could be no escape for him through the alleyway. The afternoon's events had shown clearly on which side he was, and the crowd was out for his blood. A low wicker fence divided the stable yard from the fields which stretched eastwards down to the Ouse. Tugging his horse round Brookestone set him straight at the fence. The horse responded and over they went followed by their companions.

"Follow them!" boomed the Vicar. In a few moments several horses were found for the pursuit, though an impartial observer would have pronounced them fitter for pulling wagons than running races. Eager riders mounted. The wicker fence was pulled aside, for clearly these horses were not steeplechasers, and through they thudded, led by the Vicar of Lindfield himself, his cloak flying out behind like great black wings. Cheering villagers watched the two parties and to them it seemed that Brookestone's half-mile lead was gradually being shortened by the enthusiastic galloping of the pursuers. Then the hunt was lost to view in the trees by the river. Eyes were still straining for a further glimpse of the chase when a pistol shot rang out. Silence fell on the villagers. The pursuers must be up with the pursued and only Brookestone had a pistol. No more was seen or heard of the chase and the villagers began to discuss excitedly the events of the evening, events that were to provide a topic of conversation for many years to come.

Inside the Tiger lay the dead body of Simon Jackson, robber and murderer of Nicholas Mole, poisoned by his own hand, while in another room Peter Virley tended Woodruff while he awaited the arrival of Doctor Nicol.

Twenty minutes later a clatter of hooves by the Church caused yet another stir in the village. A small detachment of dragoons under the command of Major Cheal-Herbert wheeled into the stable yard of the Tiger.

As Woodruff had feared, they had arrived too late. The birds had flown.

14

For two hours Andrew had searched feverishly. His anxiety was growing fast. Neither the cupboard nor the chest nor the table yielded the document he was looking for, and he knew that every minute of fruitless searching brought his enemy nearer. He looked round wildly. Where else? His eyes lit on a small drawer almost hidden under the top of the table. He wrenched fiercely at it. With a snap the lock gave way and the drawer shot out. He pulled out the contents, mainly yellowing parchment scrolls, and his tired eyes scanned each one with care as he held it up to the lantern. Line after line of legal phraseology written in flowing copperplate danced before his eyes. A sense of hopelessness began to steal over him. What chance had he of finding a slip of paper among this treasury of documents? He stopped searching. He must think clearly. Surely Carson held the key to all this. What had he been doing here? All the evidence suggested that he too had been searching. Had his quest been for the same scrap of paper? If so, had he been successful? Did it mean that Carson was one of the plotters?

Hardship and danger Andrew was learning to bear; but uncertainty he found more grievous than either; the more so as his best friend was concerned. As questions flooded in upon him, it was almost with relief that he heard footsteps in the street and a fumbling at the door below. He hastily threw his cloak over the uncovered lantern, conscious that the rays must have been visible through the window, and then upending the heavy table he took up a position behind it. The footsteps ascended the stairs. Andrew pulled out his pistol, already primed, and resting it on the top of the table pointed it carefully at the door. To hide would be useless. He must make the most of his advantage in position. The footsteps reached the top of stairs.

"Stay where you are," shouted Andrew, his voice firm. "If you open the door, I shoot."

There was a moment of silence outside, and then with a crash the door burst open and a light shone into the darkness of the room. Andrew's finger, trembling on the trigger, moved. An explosion echoed round the wall, the bullet tore into the woodwork just above the door, showering splinters into the room before burying itself in a thick oak beam. A laugh came from outside.

Andrew shuddered, partly with annoyance at his mistake in firing too soon and partly with fear. He knew the owner of the laugh. A figure appeared in the doorway. It was the man who called himself Dr. Carter, the man whom Andrew regarded as the murderer of Daniel. His dark eyes gleamed in the light, and his smooth olive face looked to Andrew inexpressibly evil. A levelled pistol gleamed motionless in his hand. He spoke calmly as though he were bored. "You English have an expression, 'He who laughs last, laughs longest,' I think. A good expression and an apt one, my young friend. You have had your laugh, and now it is my turn, and my laugh will be the last laugh. For you it's not laughter but prayers, and outside the true Church even those will avail you little." He pronounced each word with that deliberateness with which most foreigners treat the English language.

Andrew shuddered. This calmness chilled him. He

was crouching low behind the table with his sword drawn, working out his position. While he remained behind the table Carter could have little chance of success with his pistol, and there was only four yards between them. With one spring Andrew could reach him and cross swords with him. But that pistol! He must play for time.

"I've found nothing," he said, not finding it difficult to sound afraid. "This room had already been searched and the paper must have been taken." He knew it was useless to try to bluff about his purpose in coming, but as he said these last words he risked a peep at his adversary and saw his eyes flash towards the cupboard in the wall which he had already searched. Andrew retired behind his table, well satisfied.

"It's unwise to lie in your last moments on earth," sneered Carter. "The paper has not been taken, though I believe you when you say you have not got it. Nevertheless you know too much, and for that you must die. My shooting is more accurate than yours. You must take lessons—ah, but I am sorry. How tactless of me! You will hardly have time for that." Andrew realized the purpose of this seemingly aimless banter. It was to goad him into leaving his shelter, to make him lose his nerve. And Andrew knew how nearly it was succeeding.

Carter continued, "Now where shall I send the bullet, the head or the heart? The head I think makes a cleaner end, and all mess I abhor. That table makes a poor shield at this range." Andrew realized, however, that though the table might be ineffective as a shield it was excellent as camouflage. No marksman can be sure of hitting a head he cannot see and Carter could not afford to miss. He heard Carter moving into the room, attempting to slip round his flank. Andrew turned his table accordingly and as he did so an idea struck him.

Slowly and with some effort, for the table was good solid oak, he began to push the table towards his opponent.

Carter was slow in countering this manoeuvre. He hoped in vain that Andrew would look from behind the table, but Andrew pushing and praying hard did not look. When the table was almost on him Carter leaped to the left. Andrew wrenched the table over in that direction. It crashed on Carter's arm just as he fired. The bullet tore into the floor a yard from Carter's foot.

Half stunned by the blast of the explosion Andrew flung himself at his enemy, whose sword was not yet drawn, but the table, hitherto his friend, tripped him as he lunged forward and turned what might have been a mortal thrust into a harmless push, which Carter avoided easily

When Andrew regained his feet his advantage was lost; his opponent was in the middle of the room between Andrew and the door. His sword was flicking lightly in his hand. His lips curled in a slight grin, a contemptuous one.

"A change of weapons will not save you," he said coolly before Andrew rushed forward. All that he had learnt from Daniel went into his first onslaught, and only a swordsman of quality could have survived, but swordsman of quality Dr. Carter was. He gave ground slightly as with mere flicks of the fingers he parried and turned Andrew's thrusts. Both fencers soon appreciated the skill of their opponent and yet both were confident. Dr. Carter's mission in life had made a sword a constant and tried companion, and many young men as lithe and fierce as Andrew had met untimely deaths at his hands. He had little doubt that before two minutes were out Andrew would have joined their number.

Andrew was equally confident. He had longed for an opportunity of settling scores with Daniel's murderer. He was young and fit and skilful with the sword. He would not miss his opportunity. He attacked again.

Dr. Carter defended deftly, his eyes watching Andrew's

unwaveringly. When a lunge from Andrew went close he was able to say in the same calm voice, "A swordsman of promise."

Andrew, slightly breathless from the sudden exertion, did not reply. Dr. Carter continued,

"It is sad that one with such skill and courage should ...." The sentence was never finished. With hardly a flicker of his eyelids a vicious thrust whipped towards Andrew. It was an old ruse and Andrew was almost taken in. Desperately he turned the thrust away. It ripped his clothes and grazed his ribs, but he learnt his lesson. There was no relaxing in this fight, no gentleman's code of behaviour. It was a fight to the death. In Doctor Carter's eyes there was no mercy. The exchanges grew fiercer and faster. Andrew was forced to give ground. Beads of perspiration bedewed his brow, his heart thumped wildly, but still he was confident. He noted that Dr. Carter's calmness was evaporating. A wilder look had come into his eyes and he had no breath left for conversation.

Andrew withstood the onslaught. He had never fenced like this before and now he drove the Doctor back. Relentlessly and grimly he attacked. A faint and quick thrust nearly pierced the Doctor's guard, but he leapt back just in time to save his skin from the cold steel. As he jumped he kicked the lantern which was providing the dim light by which the duellists fought. The light flickered and then revived, and Andrew, who had automatically stood back as his opponent had stumbled, was almost taken by surprise as the Doctor sprang at him from the darkness. The light shone out just in time to allow Andrew to defend himself. The steel screeched as Andrew parried and counter-attacked. The light flickered erratically, but such was the intensity of the fight that neither of the combatants saw that the light no longer merely came from the lantern which lay broken and on its side, but from the papers, flung from the chest by the searchers, which had been lit by the naked lantern flame. They crackled merrily round the chest and a sudden glare of light flooded the room as the flames crept inside the chest.

"Fire!" gasped Andrew, and then he remembered his mission. If the fire spread the paper would be destroyed and all his efforts would be in vain. He must get it now. He had a clue, albeit a slender one. He remembered the direction of Carter's eyes at the mention of the paper, towards the cupboard protected by the portrait of James II. He had searched the cupboard and knew there was nothing there. Had he been forestalled by Carson? And then the correct solution flashed into his mind.

At the mention of the fire Carter stepped back and looked at the flames. It was too late to think of attempting to extinguish them. The chest was ablaze and the hungry tongues of fire licked greedily round the dry beams which criss-crossed the wall.

Andrew, taking advantage of the temporary truce, darted back towards the portrait and ripped the canvas. It came easily from the frame and Andrew just had time to notice that there was writing on the back of it, before Carter came at him with a fury born of desperation. Then Andrew knew he had found what he sought. The swords screeched as Andrew battled for the door. He must get to the door.

The heat of the flames and the stifling smoke were almost unbearable, but still they fought with a desperate urgency and a wild valour. Was ever such a duel as this? The clash of steel mingled in dreadful harmony with the crackle of the flames but the fighters heeded it not. Too much was at stake. Andrew had fought his way to the middle of the room when the wall by the door was suddenly engulfed in a rush of flame.

"The door," gasped Andrew, even as he warded off a frenzied hail of blows.

"Give me that paper," croaked Dr. Carter huskily, "Give me that paper." Whatever his faults he was no coward. The door was but two yards behind him. To escape then was still possible. But he stood his ground. He would not seek to escape if there was a possibility that Andrew might also escape, and that vital paper tell its tale.

The fire had now attracted an excited crowd in the street. Andrew could hear their voices as instructions were shouted. The Great Fire of London had taught Londoners a lesson they were never to forget. Gun-powder was being placed in position to demolish the adjacent houses should the fire look like spreading across the narrow alleyway, but fortunately it was a still night and what breeze there was blew the flames harmlessly out towards Ludgate. One or two braver souls, hearing the clash of steel, had ventured into the building to see if there were any who needed rescue. They were driven back by the heat and fury of the flames at the top of the stairs, comforted by the fact that no one normally slept there and that there had been ample time for escape if someone was in the office. The roar of the flames now drowned the noise of the fight.

Andrew did all he could to reach the door, but Dr. Carter implacably blocked the way, and Andrew knew that a slip on his part against such a swordsman meant death. He heard the shouts outside but they meant as little to him as the flames that crept nearer and scorched his flesh. It began to seem a dream, unreal and horrible. Surely he must soon wake up.

He saw the great beam already aflame above Dr. Carter move, wrenching itself free of the ceiling.

"The beam. Above you!" he cried automatically.

Whether Dr. Carter did not hear or whether he heard and suspected it was a trick to divert his attention we shall never know, but he disregarded the warning. He did not even glance up. Just as Andrew finished Dr. Carter lunged forward in attack again.

With a rending roar the beam tore itself from the ceiling slowly at first and then with a terrifying crunch it crashed below thudding on to the floor just behind Dr. Carter. The floor already blazing in parts was shattered by the blow. The cross beam crashed. A gaping hole was rent in the floor out of which hungry tongues of flame shot greedily. Dr. Carter felt the floor giving beneath him. Desperately he tried to spring to safety, but the planks beneath were gone. With a terrible shriek he slithered helplessly into the blazing furnace below. A Jesuit priest had died as bravely as he had lived.

Dazed and horrified Andrew staggered back, away from the door which alone held out any hope of escape now. The flames roared after him.

"Jump!" yelled a voice. "You must jump, Andrew. Jump for the door!"

The voice pulled Andrew back to reality. He must jump. He must jump that gaping mouth of fire, he must reach the door. With a tremendous effort he leaped forward and crashed on to the flaming floor. The floor began to crack and fall beneath him. He was falling.

But strong hands gripped his shoulders and pulled him from the flames.

15

It was Carson who had saved Andrew.

Three days later, as the Brighton coach bore them homewards to Lindfield, Andrew heard the story which he had longed to hear—Carson's story. Even the lurching of the coach, which sadly tortured his bruised and scorched limbs, failed to diminish the joy with which he heard the tale. He knew he had found his friend again.

Carson himself, at first pale and restrained, was soon thawed by the enthusiasm and warmth of Andrew's thanks and he told his story simply and humbly.

It had all begun when his father had decided that the profession of lawyer was the one that suited Carson best. Carson had longed to join the Army, but without his father's capital there could be no future for him there, and thus he had submitted to his father's will.

Now at this time the Tories had finally ousted the Whigs after a long term in office, and one of the main factors had been the brilliantly conducted defence of Doctor Sacheverell. One of the leading lawyers in his trial had been Talbot Brookestone, who had at once become the idol of the Tories of whom Sir Humphrey had been one. It was therefore with considerable pride that Sir Humphrey told Carson that Brookestone had agreed to act as his tutor and eventually to take him into his practice as a partner. The fees that Brookestone asked were considered by Sir Humphrey to be extremely reasonable and he had gladly granted Brookestone's request for a room in Steadwell Hall. From the first Carson had taken to his new tutor. He admired his brilliant brain and was dazzled by his knowledge and confidence in London society. Brookestone made him promises of a rosy future and Carson began to feel that the law was indeed the right profession for him. The Coffee Houses with their fine flow of conversation; the gaiety of the theatres and the excitement of the gaming houses all made his life at Lindfield seem the very essence of dullness. Carson had longed for the times when he accompanied Brookestone up to London to spend his working hours in the office near St. Paul's and his free time enjoying London's pleasures. Brookestone encouraged him in the latter as much as the former, and soon overcame Carson's scruples about gambling. Daniel Foot, his first tutor, shrank in Carson's estimation; what did Daniel know of the glories and excitement of this world? At his first night crouched at a card table he had won three pounds. By the end of that week he had doubled it. And then he was forced to return to Lindfield.

This break only served to increase his enthusiasm for cards, and when he returned it was with renewed zest and recklessness that he returned to the gaming houses. Fortune which hitherto had favoured him now deserted to his opponents. In the first week he lost more than he had gained in his successful days. Certain that his luck would return he began to draw heavily on his father's allowance. But his luck did not return. Before long he was in debt. He borrowed the money from one of the moneylenders who frequented the gaming-houses. It was only after he had borrowed and lost it that he discovered that he must pay interest at the terrible rate of forty per cent. In his desperation he dare not go to his father who, although generous in his allowance to Carson, had always made it clear that he would not overstep it by one farthing, and anyway the last thing that he wanted was that his family should know. In the end he decided to tell Brookestone; at least he felt he would not receive a sermon, for it had been Brookestone who had introduced him to the gaming table. The lawyer's response exceeded all Carson's expectations. He had paid off the debt of one hundred and twenty pounds and had even supplied Carson with fifty pounds to tide him over till the next instalment of his father's allowance. Carson's gratitude was great, but he returned passionately to the gaming house. The fifty pounds was soon gone. Brookestone again proved a friend and supplied a further allowance without interest. Carson begged to be given a chance to show his gratitude. It was not long before he was.

It was about this time that his father had decided to retire from politics. Though a Tory, he was loyal to Anne and the Hanoverian succession, and he had been alarmed to find St. John and other Tory leaders were in what seemed to him treasonable correspondence with the Jacobite court at St. Germain. Thus he resolved to return to the more peaceful and honest life of a country squire.

Jacobite hopes were again running high in England. Many Roman Catholic priests were slipping across the Channel in one disguise or another and acting as messengers between the Pretender's Court and his many supporters in England. One morning Brookestone called Carson into his private office. He told Carson that at last a chance had come for him to show his gratitude. He had a task for him which if successfully completed would mean the cancelling of all debts. Carson eagerly asked that the task be named.

Brookestone then explained that some important papers not unconnected with politics had been stolen from the office by two soldiers, whom he suspected to be Jacobite agents. He had found out that they were leaving for Sussex on the next day, doubtless with the intention of making a rendezvous on the coast and sailing to France. He had approached the Army authorities but they had offered no help and had laughed at his suspicions. He wanted Carson to attack the coach in the guise of a highwayman. Carson was taken aback at this strange request, but felt he could hardly do anything but agree. Brookestone promised him an accomplice with good local knowledge, and here Carson had his second surprise for it turned out to be none other than the landlord of the Tiger.

The plan was successfully carried through, though the shock and horror of finding his father in the coach almost unnerved him. However, the mask and his father's deafness had saved him from being detected. But he was so shaken by this episode that he left the second robbery of the papers to his accomplice.

As they had ridden back to Lindfield, Simon Jackson had been unusually talkative, possibly on account of the substantial reward offered to him if he was successful in handing over the papers to Brookestone. He began to talk politics and gradually a horrified Carson had realized that far from helping to foil the plot of traitors he himself was on the traitors' side. He had hidden his reaction from the landlord with difficulty. His mind was hopelessly confused. He had decided that he must seek advice.

Later that morning he had met Andrew in Lindfield and had almost told him the whole story, but his courage had failed him. However, after welcoming his father, a sense of shame had overcome him. How hypocritical he was being towards a father who loved him! He had rushed to Daniel, and after having made him promise not to reveal their conversation to anyone had told him everything and asked his advice. Daniel had given it, and had told Carson that he should tell Sir Humphrey and that he should leave Brookestone at once.

At this point in his story Carson's voice faltered. This part of the story was hard to contemplate in view of what followed, but Andrew, wincing as the coach lurched into a deep pothole, quietly urged him to continue. Carson went on.

He had then walked back to Steadwell Hall attempting to see clearly the issues at stake. The effect of his conversation with Daniel was great. He recalled how not many years before, thanks to Daniel's patient teaching, he had first trusted Jesus Christ as his Saviour and had for a time served Him joyfully. Those had been good days. He began to see his present life in its true light and a wave of disgust swept over him. He would break with Brookestone and begin again. He would join the Army and pay off all his debts.

He had entered Steadwell Hall, almost cheerfully, and then had come face to face with Brookestone who had beckoned Carson to follow him. They had gone to Brookestone's room, Carson willingly enough, for he had thought that this interview would give him the opportunity of breaking away from Brookestone once and for all.

Rather nervously he had told the thin-lipped lawyer of his talk with Daniel and of his decision. Brookestone heard him in a calm but ominous silence. His eyes seemed to Carson to be boring through him. Then he replied—and his reply was terrible. He pointed out that Carson had taken part in a highway robbery. The gallows was the price to be paid if he were caught. When Carson protested that he had taken part in the robbery only because he had been assured that the soldiers were traitors, Brookestone had merely laughed and had observed that he would find it hard to prove to the magistrates. And then Brookestone's voice had grown ice cold. "And the magistrates shall have enough evidence to hang you three times over, unless I have instant and absolute obedience." Carson saw Brookestone in his true light too late. Fear gripped him. Wildly he babbled he was willing to serve Brookestone in anything. For a full and dreadful minute the lawyer had surveyed him grimly and then, as if satisfied, he had unfolded the fiendish plot of the snuff-box designed to implicate Daniel and to delay the officers' investigations. He had then led Carson to the quarry, had shown him the hiding-place of the arms and had further brought him into subjection. In this way had Brookestone made it quite clear to Carson that his fortunes stood or fell with the success or failure of the plot. As they returned from the quarry Brookestone told him he must place the silver snuff-box in Daniel's house. It was a master stroke on the lawyer's part, for as well as providing a false trail he reckoned that it would completely snap Carson's loyalty to his old master, Daniel. Some of Carson's spirit returned at this suggestion and he protested with some warmth. But with the skill of a virtuoso, Brookestone played unerringly on the right strings; the theme was the gallows. A sharp look at Brookestone's face assured Carson that this was no idle threat. His defiance crumpled into a sullen assent.

As he told the story of the way he broke into Daniel's house, Carson did not dare to meet Andrew's eyes. Shame welled up in him and he thought he could expect nothing but disgust to be shown by Andrew at his revelation, but he was wrong. In his heart of hearts Andrew had long known whom he had encountered that night, and had long forgiven him.

It is to Carson's credit that he tried neither to hide nor to whitewash. He told Andrew of the horror of the days that followed. His life appeared to him broken. That day he had spent in gambling desperately with what money he had in an attempt to forget, and he had finally resolved to leave London, get across to Holland and join the army there. First he had decided he must retrieve the documents which related to his debt to Brookestone. He knew they would be used by the lawyer to drag the money from his father, and this Carson could not bear to think of. Thus when Andrew had arrived he had been ransacking the office for those papers, but his search was in vain. Despairingly he had returned to his lodging not far from St. Paul's and tried to sleep, but sleep too had deserted him. He tossed tormented and then with a sudden resolution had thrust on his clothes and returned to the office. He must find those papers!

As he approached the office he heard excited cries and saw lanterns bobbing up and down the usually black streets. He guessed it must be the Mohocks, but soon saw he was wrong. The office was ablaze. His first reaction was a purely selfish one of joy. Those papers would be burnt.

"I saw a man in the flames," screamed a woman in the crowd beside him. Carson started.

"A man? That's impossible. They're offices. No man lives there." There was a murmur of assent from the crowd.

"I tell you, I saw a man. See there...." Her words were drowned by a crash of falling timber. The crowd drew back as sparks flew among them. But Carson had seen enough. As the woman had pointed Carson had had a glimpse of a face through the window. It was Andrew's. He rushed forward to the door. A man grabbed him. "Are you mad? It's death in there."

Carson tore himself free, and shielding his face threw open the door and rushed up the stairs. Flames leapt around him, but the stairs were still firm. The heat beat fiercely at him, the smoke tried to choke him, but he reached the threshold of the office.

He was just in time to save Andrew. He half dragged and half carried his friend's body down the stairs and into the street. The crowd cheered. Andrew was unconscious, but while he was tended the woman who had first seen him in the flames noticed with interest that clasped in his left hand was what looked like a charred portrait of the late king and she soon found out that unconscious though he was nothing would make him let go.

* * * *

The coach rumbled up the hill into Lindfield. There was quite a crowd to welcome it. Garbled stories, many of them originating with Old Mother Willis, had credited Andrew and Carson with a wide variety of unlikely deeds, but after all, following the happenings of twenty-four hours previously, the wildest rumour would have received a good hearing. Sir Humphrey Pride welcomed them. A long interview with Lieutenant Woodruff had told him most of the story, all indeed except Carson's part, and perhaps he had guessed some of that. Carson went home with him.

Andrew climbed thankfully out of the coach, but his aching limbs did not prevent him running into the Tiger to the couch where the Lieutenant lay. He was relieved at Woodruff's appearance. Indeed it was hard to tell he had been wounded at all. He was resplendent in full dress uniform, his wig was perfect and Andrew even suspected that he detected some powder on the officer's face. Dr. Nicol, who extracted the bullet, had been surprised at the Lieutenant's insistence that the dressing should be as small as possible. Had he known Woodruff as well as Andrew did he would have realized how vital it was to have no disfiguring bulge to mar the smart lines of the uniform.

It was a happy reunion. The adventure had bound them closely together, but as they exchanged news they felt they were bound together by closer ties than that—the ties that bind those who trust Christ as their Saviour.

"Did they catch Brookestone?" asked Andrew.

"Not they!" replied Woodruff cheerfully. "And it's just as well they didn't or Lindfield might well have lacked its Vicar for yesterday's services. Not one of the Vicar's party was armed. Brookstone will be on the sea by now, I've no doubt. It's no matter. England is well rid of him."

"And the landlord?"

"Dead. Killed by the poison meant for me."

"And Captain Canting?"

Woodruff laughed heartily, and then stopped—it was too painful.

"The landlord made a great mistake with him. He took him prisoner and left him in the cellar."

"And where lies the mistake?"

"The barrels were full, and it didn't take our good Captain long to find that out. The ostler eventually told us where he was, and we found him lying flat on his back in a lake of beer. He was just about able to stay on a horse when he left with the Dragoons; but forget him, Andrew. Tell me, have you heard this?" And he picked up a Bible which had been lying open beside him on the couch. "Listen. It says, 'for I know whom I have believed and am persuaded that He is able to keep that which I have committed unto Him against that day.' Have you heard that before?"

Andrew nodded. He knew the verse well.

Woodruff turned from the Bible and looked at Andrew. "I've committed my life to Christ and those words are true of me. I want to tell you this, Andrew, because it was partly due to you. It started when I read those words of Daniel, 'the whole course of a man's life out of Christ is nothing but a continual trading in vanity.' I knew that described my life. I recognized it as worthless and selfish. I had had enough of trading in vanity. Then I saw you pray, and so I prayed. I prayed that my life would be without Christ no longer. I realized I needed a Saviour from sin and I found One. And now I can say with Paul and with Daniel and with you, Andrew, I *know*...."

And Andrew did not know what to say but he thanked God in his heart.

"Well, it's London for me to-morrow, friend. Orders arrived just before you did. Come with me. After this I think you'll be safe for a commission. I've written up a fine report for you. How would you like a uniform like this, eh?"

Andrew shook his head. He cared little about the uniform though he would dearly have liked to stay with Woodruff. He had been thinking it out and praying about it since Daniel's death and knew what his answer must be.

"Some day I may join you, but I am no soldier. I feel I've seen enough fighting to last my lifetime. My father wished that I might follow a peaceful trade. Daniel wished me to be a schoolmaster, and that is what I will be. I once thought Virgil dull, but how I long for dullness now!"

Woodruff laughed. "So be it, but before a year is out you'll be crying for the real life, the soldier's life again...."

"We shall see; but what about Carson? He's always longed to join the Army. Is there hope of a commission for him?"

"Carson? Hm, well, he's of a good family, looks well. I think there might be."

In case it appears that Woodruff was overestimating his powers of influence, it should be said that he had received a most cheering packet from London, which, based on a report of the Major of Dragoons who had arrived in Lindfield three days before, praised him lavishly and announced his promotion to Captain. When Captain Canting referred subsequently to this, he always held it to be a supreme example of favouritism and corruption in the Army, and then he would go on to recount how he almost single-handed had foiled the plotters with Lieutenant Woodruff a more or less useless hanger-on.

And so the Jacobite plot failed. Those supporters whose names were on Andrew's hard-won scroll, and who had awaited the arms in vain, were treated with a clemency unusual in those times. The details of the plot were never published abroad; perhaps Lord Bolingbroke and his supporters in the Government, whose hopes lay in a Jacobite succession, saw to that.

So we leave Andrew with his Virgil, Peter with his cows, Carson proudly setting off to join his regiment, the Reverend Thomas Bysshe, highly respected Vicar of Lindfield, with a church packed beyond his wildest dreams, and Woodruff brushing a lonely speck of dust from his perfect uniform as he strode towards the Cocoa Tree Chocolate House. Perfect uniform? Well, not quite. There was a bulge in one of his side pockets. That bulge contained a Bible.

If you have enjoyed this book, there are plenty more in the "Kingfisher" series that make exciting reading, for example,

THE MAN WITH THREE FINGERS
by J. B. Donovan.

When Dan Brent discovers that Gregory, "The Man with Three Fingers" has stolen vital documents outlining the whereabouts of a special type of crystal found only in Peru, he is desperately worried. The crystal absorbs light to such an intensity that when it is focussed on a living creature, the effect is lethal. Gregory, confident of finding the crystal, has already offered it to a rival government, who realise its evil potential.

A dangerous chase begins. Also involved are Dan's brother Mike, and Mike's friend G.B. Before the adventure ends, Mike—a Christian, has occasion to test just how much he trusts God, and G.B. learns something of commitment to a person, not a principle.

The climax is reached when Gregory joins forces with a pagan High Priest in order to defeat the representatives of law and order and bring an end to belief in God in the mountain town of Zicchu.

 Look for the Kingfisher symbol.